Soul

BY:

SKYLER
DEGROTE

This book is a work of fiction. Any references to historical events, real people, or real locales are used fictitiously. Other names, characters, places and incidents are the product of the author's imagination, and any resemblance to actual events or locales or persons, living or dead, in entirely coincidental.

Cover art design by Skyler DeGrote

This book is dedicated to my mom and dad for being there for me throughout the process. I would also like to thank all of my friends whom have given me the support, and encouragement along the way. It's because of all of you that I have been so committed to completing this book.

Chapter 1

Kate Sanders strode into the club wearing a low-cut, bright red leather shirt and sexy black leather pants. This was the normal outfit for a night out on the job. Her sisters, Julie and Sadie, didn't know where she was. Six hours previously, she had told them she was heading out to the grocery store. Of course they knew something was up because Kate didn't normally go to the grocery store in a full leather outfit.

I'm just going to look around for some potential threats, Kate thought to herself. Really, if nothing happened with this Tyson guy, she wanted some type of action. *Maybe I can get some information out of some weaklings. There has to be more than just this Tyson guy that knows something about a demon with a large soul collection.*

Kate looked around the club as she approached the open bar stool. It was a decent looking club with demons and humans from everywhere around the world welcome. They came to sit and chat with no violence between them allowed. As the bartender greeted her, she noted the layout of the club. There was a dance floor and round tables, with four chairs surrounding the open area. The bar was long and straight with a stone counter. There was only one bartender on duty tonight. *Hopefully he's my guy,* Kate thought.

"Hello, pretty lady. Would you like a drink?" he smiled.

Kate just smiled and nodded. "I'll have a Cosmo."

"What's a small town girl like you doing in a club like this?" the bartender asked.

Kate noticed his name tag. *Perfect,* she thought. His name was Tyson.

The truth was that Kate had gone to the grocery store to meet a demon out back who had owed her a favor. He'd told her that a vampire named Tyson worked at the club called Mixed, and that Tyson was the one she'd want to talk to. He supposedly had as much information about The Devil as possible.

"I'm actually from around here," Kate told Tyson. "But to answer your question, I like clubs like this. I find it to be an interesting experience every time."

"Fair enough," he replied. "What's your name, honey?"

"You know, I'm surprised you don't recognize me." Kate started, her tone as confident as she felt, "I'm the leader of the group that put The Devil in Hell a long time ago." She bluffed. True, Kate was the leader of the 666 group, but it was her ancestor, Kate Sanders, that locked the gate to Hell after The Devil's greed for power overthrew him- not her.

My family goes way back to the early 1800s and it's a little confusing. We were always triplets and always named the same in the same order. Kate is the one that always reproduces, and she always has triplets and dies with childbirth. The first of the triplets born is always Kate and she always acts the same towards people. She's always the leader of our family. So Kate always dies during childbirth and our dad is never part of our life in some way or another. Sadie is always the second born. She is the strength and the brains of the group. In every generation she gets stronger and smarter when it comes to fighting.

She despises all things evil and loves that we kill them for a living. I'm always the last-born and I'm always the witch. But there is more to me than just being the witch.

We are the thirteenth generation of the Sanders' demon hunters. Being a witch means that with each generation, I get more powerful quicker because I was born with more power as time goes on. How I die each time is the same and it's because of Kate giving childbirth meaning she's not out on the battlefield.

At six years of age, the three of us find a note that was written by our mother. The note contained a lot of information that we need in order to understand our role in this world.

— — —

Demons, vampires, ghouls and most importantly The Devil all exist.
You are the 666 group. Our family has been for …a while.
You must help keep The Devil in Hell by killing these demons.

Julie, a powerful witch is what you are and will become. Here is a copy of Spells Introduction.

Sadie, you are strong and I don't want you to ever forget that. Here is a book on self defense.

Kate, be a leader, do your best and I know you girls will succeed.

Kill the demons and defeat The Devil.

Have fun and protect each other.

— — —

Generation after generation the Sander Triplets get stronger and wiser. The current generation has some extras that they have to deal with along with the usual Sanders' way of the life of killing demons.

"You aren't really part of the 666 group, are you? You look too innocent to have murdered all those demons."

The 666 group got their name because of the curse that was put upon The Devil thirteen generations ago. The first generation of the Sanders' triplets were the ones to put Sage in his own Hell dimension with a curse put on him so he could not get out of Hell unless he collected six hundred and sixty six souls by killing people. He found a loop hole so he didn't have to kill each person but instead he turns them into demons, vampires, ghouls and ghosts; but he stuck with mostly vampires. The curse that the first generation 666 group put on Sage was actually known as the '666 curse'. This is why the number 666 is normally referred to when talking about The Devil or evil or something of that matter. It was a very powerful curse with no back ways out. Sage was truly stuck and therefore the girls that put him in his own Hell were named after the curse that kept him down there. Sometimes the Sanders girls are known as The Devil Family or the Triple 6 Family but the most common reference to them is the 666 group.

"Looks can be deceiving. Now do you know who I am?" His eyebrows rose to a high position of surprise and disbelief. Then he seemed to come to his senses and agree that she could, in fact, be part of the murderous group. After all, the 666 group members were supposed to try to blend in. He smiled and nodded. "Good," Kate continued. "Now let's get to it. Your name is Tyson, correct?" He nodded again. "I have some questions for you, Tyson. I require the truth. Shall we finish this conversation out in the open where anyone can hear us, or would you rather save your business and step outside with me?" Kate saw Tyson's expression and read it as intimidated but Kate also knew that someone like Tyson was probably good at hiding expressions such as comprehension of why she was in his club that night.

"I don't see a reason to leave," Tyson said. "It's not like I have anything to hide."

"Alright. I just didn't want some of your best customers to hear about the club you owned in California and how you burned it to the ground with all your customers blocked inside." The guy sitting next to Kate now had wide eyes. Kate noticed Tyson's face growing furious.

"She's lying, Joey," Tyson told the man. "I never owned another club called Mixed, and I've never been to California."

"But there were news stories about a club in California that was burned down with all it's costumers inside, Tyson." the demon replied. "How can anyone be sure it wasn't *your* club?"

Instead of answering the frightened customer, Tyson turned to Kate and smiled widely. "You and I shall go out back"

Kate knew that expression all too well from other demons she had threatened using their business and customers. It was a low blow, but it always worked. She smiled and stood up from her bar stool, leaving her drink on the stone counter, following the bartender to the employee door and out back.

What does she think, That I'm stupid? I wouldn't burn a bar down in California, and then name a club as the same name afterwards. That would just be stupid. That would probably be what Tyrone would do. Anyway, I knew someone from the demon hunting job would come to my club eventually. And I'm just surprised, no change that to pleasantly surprised, that it was someone from the 666 group. It's an honor to be such a threat to society that they have to send their best. That group really is the best at the demon hunting stuff. They don't need any equipment. I mean they even have their own witch running along with them. And damn are these girls HOT. They make vampires want to drool on them before going for their throats. They make us weak. Some vampires would even probably let them go with only a cut to prove they were bitten because of the fame and beauty these girls have. I love that it was Kate, the leader, that showed up too. I never knew these girls did separate jobs; I thought they were always together on the job. Maybe Sadie and Julie are somewhere in the distance as back up if Kate needs it. Though it doesn't seem like she does. But I have a little surprise for you oh-graceful-one. Tyson thought as they walked out to the alley way.

They exited the club and walked through an

alleyway for a couple minutes. Kate looked around. The alleyway was lit up by one street lamp that was flickering on and off in the distance. There were hundreds of places that other people or demons could be hiding around the corners. Buildings with vines going up the sides surrounded them. Kate was freaked at the moment but the fear passed at once. *I can't show any fear because then he'll know that he can scare me by being alone with me. That would be the worst situation ever!* Kate thought as they continued through the dark area. When Tyson was sure that they were alone, he invited his friends to come out of the shadows. Kate was not surprised at what she found as they stopped walking. Tyson had been expecting her to show up, so he was prepared with three strong vampire guards.

"They won't be necessary, Tyson," she said. "I just have a few questions and I'll be on my way." The three guards came closer to her, one blocking her way back into the club and the others grasping her forearms tightly.

"You won't be going anywhere unless you cooperate with how I want to do things- my way," Tyson replied. "You are a hunter?" Kate nodded. "And you hunt demons?" Another nod. "Were you in my club tonight on a job?" Kate shook her head. "Then why were you here tonight?" Tyson pressed.

Am I intimidating her right now? Or is that just an act? Tyson thought.

"To have a couple drinks and relax." Kate was lying, but she hoped that Tyson couldn't tell.

"You aren't lying to me, are you? I think you would like it better if you just told me the truth. I would have to hurt you if you were giving me false answers." Tyson stepped closer to Kate and she scrambled to back up.

Kate was suddenly filled with a fear she had never felt before. Tyson wasn't really that intimidating but she could see that she was in a tough spot. *I really should not have come with no backup.*

"I swear, I just wanted to have fun tonight. Why else would I come with no backup?" Kate thought this was a good point to bring up since it was a fact. Yet, Tyson knew all too well that the really good hunters had their backup hiding somewhere in the distance- close enough to come to the rescue, but far enough to stay unnoticed.

Kate didn't have the patience to wait for her sisters. They were at the spa when she went back home from the grocery store. She just wanted to get the job over with, and that's why she showed up with no backup. Mistake number one. Mistake number two was telling Tyson that she in fact had no back up.

"No backup? Not even a boyfriend?" Tyson proceeded.

"I... I don't have a boyfriend. I don't have time for that kind of stuff," Kate commented.

Why does he care if I have a boyfriend? It's not like I would ever date him. And even if I did have a boyfriend, I wouldn't let him in on this half of my life. I would probably lead a double life more so then I do now. But why does Tyson care?

"Hmmm, that's interesting."

"Why is that interesting?"

"You didn't come here tonight to just hang out," Tyson answered. "You wouldn't have come straight to the bar like you did. You would have looked around a little more. You had another reason for coming tonight and you are going to tell me what the reason is."

"I don't know what you're talking about," Kate lied.

"If you came here to just have fun, why did you go straight for *me* at the bar? And why are you dressed like this? That looks like a slutty on-the-job outfit," Tyson claimed, giving Kate the up-down.

"It is, but that doesn't mean..." Kate started but Tyson gave her the death glare and, in her current position, it could be just that. One of the guards was forcing her neck to the side and holding her rust-colored red hair out of the way. At any moment, any one of the four vampires could kill her instantly if they wanted to, and she wouldn't be able to do anything about it.

"Tyson, I just want to go home. I won't come to your club anymore. I won't cause any more trouble. Please, just let me go home."

"You aren't going anywhere until I get answers."

"What do you want to know? I'll answer any question." Kate instantly regretted that idea.

Tyson smiled and took another step closer to Kate until they were only a foot apart. "I think we should continue this in my office," he sneered. Kate started to shake her head in disagreement, but the vampires just pulled her with them.

I could scream and make a bunch of noise for Tyson's customers to hear. What would he do to me if I did that? Kate asked herself. She knew it wasn't the best idea, but she started to anyway.

"Somebody help me, please! Help! Somebody!" Kate's mouth was covered by one of the vampires and she was forced to face Tyson. They were only halfway down the long staircase and Tyson didn't look happy. *I knew that wasn't a smart idea,* she cursed her decision.

"Shut up!" Tyson yelled as Kate tried to scream

again. "Don't make me hurt you!" There was a trace of anger in his voice, but it was mostly a kind warning. Tyson was really trying to be a polite captor.

Tyson is tall. He's muscular and rarely hides it. Tyson has dark brown hair that tightly framed his face, and deep brown eyes. Tyson was very fond of the way he looked and he was very obviously aware of how good-looking he really was. In a way, Tyson's hair was messy but it was that type of messy that is stylish for a guy, in Kate's opinion. The muscles are the only part of Tyson that intimidated Kate. Kate had dealt with many demons that could toss her around if they wanted to, and most of them did. Tyson definitely could have tossed Kate around if he wanted to, but he refused to. For some reason, this made Kate more afraid of him instead of more confident with her own strength.

"If you let me go," Kate said, "I won't scream anymore. You can't just keep me here."

"Yes I can," Tyson smiled. "Who's going to know? The only people who are going to miss you are your sisters. They won't know where to find you, so I have all the time in the world to keep you here. I wasn't planning on it, but we could make this work."

The 666 group had always in history been three girls, always triplets and always the same names. Every demon ever made, especially if they were made by Sage, like Tyson was, knew about the Sanders girls. They were basically trained to have the knowledge of these girls. Tyson knew that Kate's sisters wouldn't go looking for her unless they had proof that something was up and even then, Kate was the one with the connections of places- not them so how would they know where to go? All demons made by Sage knew that Kate was the leader and that Sadie and Julie were her sisters but they were also just sidekicks.

"What do you want to know? I will tell you anything." Kate's fear was extended because of the position of her neck as they stood in the office in the basement of the club. The guards holding her now had her neck fully to the side and her hair out of the way. The one guard had his fangs popped out and ready for the bite as soon as Tyson gave him the go.

"Tell me why you came here tonight." Kate swallowed hard.

Chapter 2

"I already told you. I came to have fun."

"After that."

"What?"

"You had a purpose. You came in, you looked around carefully, as though trying to find someone. Who were you trying to find?"

"Fine. I'll tell you." Kate barked as the guards started to tilt her head and lean in. She was starting to freak out. Tyson had given them the okay to bite unless she objected with information, "Earlier today I went to the grocery store to meet someone with information. You might know him, his name is Gust." Tyson's eyes grew wide, "He told me that a vampire named Tyson worked at the club named Mixed and had the information I was looking for on a specific demon. I came to the club, not getting my hopes up, but then when I sat at the counter you were the one that took my order. Once I saw your name on your nametag, I knew it had to be you and I knew I had to get the information while I had the chance. I was supposed to wait for my back up but my sisters are at the spa and I was bored so I went with it. Now I see it was a bad idea, so can I just go and get out of your life and..." Kate attempted to leave again.

"You leave now and I'll just come find you. What will happen if I find one of your sisters instead of you? Would you like to endanger your family as well?"

"No, but... but you can't just hold me against my will. That's kidnapping!"

"What's your point, Kate? Kidnapping is one of the things that vampires, like myself, are good at."

"I'll call the police. I'll cause your costumers to not come anymore. I'm stronger than you think, I'll kill you." Kate ran out of threats. Tyson started laughing at Kate when she stopped making the empty threats. The tone in her voice was weak. She didn't believe that she could do any of those things anymore than Tyson believed it.

"Your threats are empty. You know right now that if you tried any of that, you would regret it instantly. Four vampires against one hunter. It would be way too easy to overpower you." Tyson exclaimed. The two guards let Kate go at Tyson's command to do so and Kate backed up into the wall as Tyson walked closer to her. He trapped her against the wall and made it so only an inch separated them, "Tell me what I want to know." Kate nodded. She, honestly, had no other choice but to cooperate now. To say at the least, Kate was afraid of what Tyson might do to her. What Kate didn't know, is that Tyson may be a vampire but he wasn't going to harm a 666 group member; at least not yet. She was exactly what he needed to set his boss free. But if she was afraid, Tyson could use that to his advantage. Tyson put his hands on the wall of the basement on either side of Kate so she was blocked from even an attempt to escape. Tyson's face was almost touching Kate's and Kate was still trying to back away from him.

"I will. I'll tell you anything you want to know."

21

"Good girl." He smiled and put his legs on the out sides of hers to make it even less likely for her to escape, "What did Gust tell you about me?"

"He just told me that you would have some, if not all, of the information I want about another demon that my sisters and I are hunting right now."

demons come and go for Kate and her sisters. Going after all of the demons in the world at once would just be too difficult for the Sanders girls so they have to focus on one demon at a time. One demon catches their attention and then they spend all of their time and energy on researching that demon. Sometimes it'll take a day to kill it and sometimes it'll take months. If the demon is a vampire, they have different rules. They wait to see if the vampire plans to kill the human they are biting. If the vampire is only taking blood to survive and not to kill, the girls will cut a deal with it. They'll make the demon swear on their blood that they will never bite to kill, only to survive. Swearing by blood even if you are a demon is permanent. They drop dead -the true dead- if they break the agreement. This way, if the girls let a vampire go because they are only trying to survive, they won't regret it later. What they didn't know is that there was a back way out of that blood-sworn agreement.

"I spared him three times now, when seeing him attacking an innocent human. He owed me a favor, actually three favors, and so I told him to meet me out back of the grocery store and to have the information available." Kate explained.

"What demon are you after right now?"

"I don't know his name. I only know his killing streak. Gust said you would have his location and name."

"What is his killing streak then?"

"It might have increased since my last update of information but last time I looked, it was 613. He's collecting souls. I think he might be the demon that my ancestors cursed but I'm not sure."

Kate barely knew the past of her ancestry and she wasn't showing it off to Tyson at all. At this point, Tyson knew that he knew more about Kate's family's past than she did. *Doesn't she know why she is a Hunter by blood?* Tyson asked.

"You speak of The Devil?" The guard that said this sounded surprised. The two guards were standing by the stairs now, making sure that if Kate got past Tyson, she wouldn't be able to get out of the basement.

"The Devil? What! Seriously? My ancestors put The Devil in Hell?"

"Yes. Sage is his human name. Why are you after The Devil and what makes you think you can kill him? It's almost impossible." Tyson's eyebrows were high on his forehead again.

Kate can be clueless. She knows that The Devil exists, and she knows that she is a demon hunter but Kate is a little lacking in the knowledge about who her ancestors put in Hell thirteen generations previously. She's unsure of the past of her family. Kate was very surprised that it was in fact The Devil that her ancestors trapped and cursed all those years ago and that her and her sisters were going after now.

"Well now that I know he's The Devil, I know it might be harder than we expected. Do you know any tips on easier ways to kill him?"

"Not that I'm going to tell you. You'll have to do your own research on that. What do you know about him?" Tyson told Kate, sounding a little surprised himself. Tyson couldn't believe that his boss was being chased by the future version of the girls that put him in Hell in the first place. He was so close to getting out;

only less than a hundred souls left to collect. But the curse got more complicated as Sage got closer to getting out. The last hundred souls had to be from willing people under a normal conversation's circumstance.

"I don't know anything except his killing streak." Kate commented. Tyson noticed the blue eyes staring into his brown ones. He never noticed that Kate had waist length rusty red hair, bright blue eyes and the most beautiful facial features he'd seen in a long time. Kate's nose was shorter than normal, her mouth curled up in a grin even as she became more frightened and her cheeks were naturally rosy. Kate was tanner than other girls that Tyson had bitten from but he wasn't very surprised.

Mostly vampires, but other types of demons as well, are judged in the demonic world by how many people they kill. Sage has the highest kill streak and he's not even a demon, but no one except Tyson knows this.

"How did you know Gust would have information on Sage?" Tyson asked, now just out of pure curiosity.

"I didn't, honestly. That was pure luck. And

besides, he didn't have information on Sage, he just knew who would." Kate specified.

"How come I don't believe that?"

"Because you don't want to. You don't want to believe I can tell a threatening vampire the truth to save my life. You think that just because you have me trapped down here with no chance of escaping that I would lie in order to get out. I'm telling you the truth. Gust told me nothing other than that you would have the information about Sage. I called him up and asked him if he knew of a demon with a large kill streak of more than six hundred. He said he could help out and so we met and talked. He didn't give me anything more than that, I swear." Kate tried to back up into wall even more but it was hopeless. Even if she could, Tyson would only scoot closer to her against the wall.

"You can relax Kate." Tyson commented on Kate's now stiff legs and arms. "I'm not going to kill you. You are too much fun to mess with. I like scaring you into thinking I'll hurt you, but the truth is that I wouldn't dare hurt a girl with such power. Why do that, when I could just keep you here as a slave all to myself?"

"You will not keep me here as your slave!" Kate

demanded.

"Relax, sweet heart. No need to worry. I plan to let you go as soon as I'm done collecting information."

"What other information do you need? I *have* nothing else!"

"Yes you do. Why did you choose to keep going with the mission even without back up? Did you think it was going to be easy getting information about The Devil out of me?"

"I didn't expect to be captured like this, if that's what you are asking. I thought that maybe I could just ask a few questions and leave without any suspicion. I was wrong. But is that all you need? Because if I don't get home soon, or at least call, my sisters are going to come search for me. This bar is the first place they'll look. What else do you want from me?" Kate knew that she was probably wrong. Her sisters wouldn't know where to start looking. They knew why she was taking so long but she wasn't answering her cell and she didn't leave a note so they would be clueless as to where to start looking for her.

"I want you to stay around for a while. Just in case I come up with more questions to ask. How about we put you to work upstairs? Sound like a decent idea?"

Tyson stepped away from Kate and Kate relaxed a little after he took a couple steps back. Kate took a minute to evaluate her captor. He was tall and slender. Tyson was wearing a blue long sleeve shirt with the logo for the bar on the pocket with black work-like pants. The collar of Tyson's shirt was folded up and Kate took another moment to notice that he had dark brown eyes that stewed as dim as the mud on the ground after a long shower of rain. His dark brown hair tightly wrapped around his features and somehow made his skin look a lot tanner than it really was.

"No! I'm not your slave! I'm not going to work for you!"

"You will if I threaten you. Does it have to come to that?"

"You just told me that you won't hurt me or kill me so why should I believe that I should be afraid of your threats?"

"I told you I wouldn't kill or harm *you*." Tyson corrected Kate. He raised his eyebrows at her and she swallowed hard.

"You don't know where I live. You can't come

through with that threat either. My family is safe as long as they stay in our home."

"Will they though? You said that they'd come try to find you. If this is the first place they'll look, I could hurt them pretty easily." Tyson said. He had a good point.

"I'm sorry, but am I allowed to laugh at that? My sisters are a lot stronger than even I know. They would be able to take you out in two seconds. You couldn't beat Julie, alone, if you tried."

"Oh? You think so? Why's that?"

"She's a witch. A very powerful witch." Kate claimed.

"Well we'll see about that. Come on, Kate. You are my newest waitress. Welcome to the team." Tyson shoved a blue uniform into Kate's hands after one of the guards handed it to him, "Your shift starts in five minutes. Be up there for training or be punished." Tyson warned, "Don't push your luck, Kate Sanders." Tyson had a big smile on his face as he waited for Kate's argument statement.

"I don't want to…"

"You don't have a choice."

"There is always a choice," Kate commented quietly, "but...my choices are limited. I'll see you upstairs." She had noticed Tyson's death glare again. Kate felt like she was becoming all too familiar with that look on Tyson's face.

"Good girl. Be quick." Tyson left the room followed by the three guards. Kate stood alone in the basement. She took a few minutes to look around and noticed that it was basically an office. There was a desk in the corner with a computer and a desk chair. The walls were well decorated as well. After seeing that everything looked like a normal office, and not like a dungeon like Kate had thought it would be, she changed into the blue uniform. The uniform consisted of a tight fitting blue short sleeve shirt that was way to short and showed her midsection in full, and the shortest skirt that Kate had ever put on. She slowly walked up the stairs to find Tyson waiting at the top. *What did I get myself into?* Kate asked herself.

Chapter 3

"That color suits you." He smiled. The uniform was a light blue like the sky on a cloudless day. Kate did look good in it but it was too short and too tight. Kate's midsection was fully exposed and the skirt was only covering her underwear with about two inches of fabric. Tyson liked the look but Kate was under the impression that the uniform wasn't his biggest interest.

"No, it doesn't. You just like what you picked out for me. Was this uniform for a two year old, or something? It's way too tight for my liking!" Kate complained.

"It's not you we want to please. It's the costumers."

"I'm sure it is. Are you sure it's not *you* that this outfit is *satisfying*?"

"I think we need to focus on training you in." Tyson changed the subject as he gave Kate another head-to-toe, "Do you know how to make alcoholic drinks?"

"The ones humans drink, yes." Kate answered, "I don't understand why you are making me work for you."

"You really think I'm going to keep you here and just watch you do nothing in the basement? This way I can keep an eye on you and I get something out of it." Tyson claimed.

"What do I get out of all this?"

"You get to work for a *vampire*. Isn't that exciting?" Tyson smiled.

As Kate worked the night away, Tyson watched her talk to the customers. He critiqued her every now and again but was overall impressed with her skills. When the last customer left, Tyson asked Kate to meet him downstairs after she cleaned the tables and dance floor. Kate tried to take her time because less time near Tyson meant more time to find a way to escape. As she cleaned she surveyed the room, looking for an easy escape. There was a front door, which was locked from the outside, and a long bar covered the entire right side. Tables and seating were scattered around the center of the room, leaving the dance floor open. The only back door is the one downstairs. There is no escape. Kate realized she was re-cleaning the tables in an attempt to delay her meeting Tyson in the basement. She decided that the wise thing to do was to not keep him waiting.

Tyson tapped his foot in impatience when he saw her come down the stairs. "Last I checked, it doesn't take twenty minutes to sweep and wipe the tables." Tyson commented. Tyson was about to run up stairs to check on Kate but not because he was afraid she would get away. It would've been because he was worried someone else had come in and taken her. That was bound to happen at some point and so he had to keep a close eye on his captive.

"First day on the job. Don't want to upset the boss with my lack of cleaning skills. Just wanted to make sure I got everything spotless." Kate claimed.

"Kate, I need answers from you. Sit down,

please."

"All of a sudden you're asking nicely? What's with that?"

"Complaining about your captor being nice doesn't seem like the best idea, Ms. Sanders." Tyson said, "Now sit." This time it wasn't asked so nicely.

Kate walked over to the round table that was next to the corner desk and sat in the chair across from Tyson. Tyson smiled widely and leaned in towards Kate while she leaned back in her chair.

"Kate. Do you want to leave?" Kate didn't answer. She knew this had to be a trick, "I asked you a simple question, Kate."

"Of course I want to leave. Who wouldn't want to get away from someone that is keeping them against their will? Are you insane?"

"Kate, I'm going to make a deal with you." Kate just sat in her chair, motionless, "The deal is I will let you go in two days if you tell me everything I want to know." There was silence for a short second, "Do we have a deal?"

"What are my other options?"

"Kate. I want you to be comfortable while you are in my care."

"In your *care*? Are you seriously calling this that? You are holding me against my will and as soon as I get my fingers on a phone, I'm calling the police!" Kate threatened.

"Kate, calm down. You want to go? I'll let you leave tomorrow if you give me everything I want today. But as soon as you are hesitant on answering a question or doing a task, you are mine to keep until Saturday. Deal?"

"Fine." Kate said furiously. *Tomorrow. I'll leave tomorrow.* She thought. Something inside Kate told her that she wouldn't be leaving until Saturday. Something deep down told her that she would probably be here in Tyson's 'care' for even longer than that. And even deeper down yet something told Kate that she was going to be allowed to leave but feel like she can't because of the feelings slowly rising between her and Tyson.

— — —

"Julie, I'm worried about her." Sadie said to the witch in the family. Sadie and Julie were both still in their pajamas and sitting on their living room couch. It was Ten AM on a Thursday and neither of them cared that they weren't ready for the day. This statement got Julie to sigh though. Sadie always did know how to over-worry.

"I'm sure Kate's fine. She probably just got caught up in a job last night."

"She said she was going to the grocery store. How can she not be back from that two days later? You can't tell me you don't feel like something is wrong!"

"Alright. What do you suppose we do? Kate is a strong, independent woman. And you know I can't fight worth shit so what would be the point of searching for her?"

"Julie! You are a *witch*! Do some locater spell or something!" Julie didn't like this idea at all. Locater spells were sometimes dangerous depending on what or who you were trying to locate.

"I'm trying to meditate!" Julie started to get upset with her sisters' interruptions. Sadie didn't like that Julie wasn't interested in her other sister's safety.

"Come on! Kate is our *sister*."

"Will it make you shut up?" Sadie nodded, "Alright. Let me go get my candle."

"You don't need a candle for a locater spell…" Sadie was wondering what Julie was up to. Lately, Julie had been extra moody and extra bitchy about everything in life. It seemed to Sadie that Julie didn't care if their sister was in danger or why Kate wasn't back. Kate had gone to the grocery store two days ago and Julie hadn't at all cared that she was still gone. Sadie was the one that kept trying to call Kate, who's bag was no where to be seen since she had gotten caught by Tyson. Kate was never out this long without a phone call and Sadie was deeply worried.

"I'm not doing a locater spell. Because if you are right, and Kate is in trouble, she could be held captive somewhere and a locater spell is obvious to the people around the person it's locating. They'll see it and they could inflect harm to her if they are violent people. This is a danger-detecting spell. Invisible to anyone except the people casting it and the people it's about. She'll know right away to follow the directions that I'll be speaking. I'll be basically speaking them into her ear without knowing where she is or being there. And I'll be able to tell if she is in danger." Julie explained.

"Do you need my help?" Sadie asked.

"Yeah. I need you to sit cross-legged across from me with your hands palm side up a little past your knees. Don't say anything though." Julie commanded. Then she continued with the spell.

"Carmilla. Goddess of fear, anger, and pain. I ask that you help us seek out our sister. Please locate her and let her hear our words." Julie chanted, "It's working. Kate. Listen to me. This is Julie. Follow what I say. I am going to ask you yes or no questions. Blink once for yes, twice for no. Please do this." Julie felt a power serge through her. Kate answered with yes, "Are you being held captive?" Kate blinked once. Yes. "Are you hurt?" two blinks, "Has your captor threatened you in any way?" Yes. "Are you in our home town?" Yes. "Are you near the grocery store?" two blinks again. "Are you in a bar or restaurant or club?" Yes. "That is all I need. Thank you Kate. We will come and find you. Carmilla. Goddess of fear, anger and pain. I thank thee for thy power. I thank thee for thy help." Julie opened her eyes and noticed that her sister, in front of her, had a nosebleed and somehow was still in the spell.

The goddess of fear, anger and pain, named Carmilla, was known for leaving evidence behind, showing that someone in that room called upon her using dark magic. This type of magic was forbidden in the olden days and therefore it was looked down on in the recent century as well. Carmilla is, because she's the goddess of fear and anger and pain, very good at making the magic-user aware of the worst possible things that could be happening to whom ever they are trying to protect. Most goddesses don't believe that humans are worthy of calling upon them for help. Each goddess has their own way of making the human using magic to call upon them pay. Carmilla's way of doing this is to make the human, or a helper near by, see or feel the pain in the worst case scenario.

"Sadie? Are you okay? Come on, sis. The spell is over. Come back to Earth." That's when Sadie opened her eyes and started crying, "Sadie, what's wrong?"

"Where is she, Julie? Where is Kate? We've got to find her!"

"I promise you, we'll find her." Julie swore to her sister.

Julie was a powerful witch. More powerful than any witch known to the planet. And more powerful than the witches named Julie in her family ancestry. She was determined to learn more and more each day about controlling her powers, and using them without side effects. It was a hard task but it was worth the trouble that it caused.

"How are we going to find her? Locater spells, apparently, will give away that we are looking. We could go search for her, but there are too many bars in this town and restaurants are basically endless. There are too many clubs too! What are you going to do, to find her?" Sadie was panicking now. Julie knew that it was going to be hard for Sadie to see that and understand that the images she saw were worst-case-scenario images. This was another thing that Carmilla liked to do. Poor Sadie had to see all the things that could be happening to their sister. All the worst possible situations Kate could be in. If it were happening to Julie, she'd be panicking too. But Julie was also a little used to it so she would know it wasn't real. Sadie on the other hand didn't at all know that this was just a punishment to Julie for casting the spell; she believed everything she saw. Sadie's mind filled with flashes of Kate hanging on a wall being tortured and whipped and more images came of Kate drowning. Some truth was in these images because Sadie also saw Kate working for a vampire and not being harmed in any way; closely watched, but not harmed. These images flashed into Sadie's mind over

and over again. Then Sadie came back to reality.

"When Kate went to the store, she hinted to me that she was going there to interview someone. Look around her office. Maybe we can find something that tells us who it was that she was interrogating." Julie suggested.

Suddenly, Julie picked up a signal in her head. As a witch, if someone without the ability to get to a phone needed to get a hold of her, they could force her to hear their thoughts by specifically thinking to her. This was hard to do but being blood related made it slightly easier. The goddess of Evil Acts, or Anita, was playing a trick on Julie, though. As a witch Julie was supposed to be able to do this but not all goddesses liked the fact that humans could have the power of a witch; only because that is one step closer to being a goddess. The goddesses of the world often worked together and so if one was unpleased so were others and they all eventually put their shame on the human witch and their friends and family.

Julie. Julie could have sworn it was Kate thinking to her. *I'm in a club, not a restaurant or bar. It's called Mixed. Don't come now. I'm not in any immediate danger. They need me alive. Come tomorrow. Come at three pm on the dot. If you come today or before three pm tomorrow, he will be mad.*

This way of communicating was basically not heard of, other than for the Sanders girls. The 666 ancestry of power helped them succeed every time. Even with the ancestry's power helping Julie out with this charm, Julie had to know what she was doing when setting the charm up. The Sanders girls had a back room in their house and Julie had candles and rocks all lined up for this charm to work. Julie also had been practicing her magic and seeing how much power she really had by experimenting. This was one of the experiments; and Julie thought it was working when really The goddess of evil acts was just punishing Julie for attempting this charm of long distance mind reading by pretending to be her sister. Julie knew that there were possibilities that her sister was not the person that was speaking to her; but she just had high hopes that something like this would happen so she believed the lie.

Chapter 4

Neither Julie nor Sadie could fall to sleep knowing their sister was in some form of danger. Immediate or not, they couldn't help but worry. Julie sprung up in her bed and sat there, knowing she had to do something- anything.

Sadie woke up suddenly with tears already running down her cheeks. Not because Julie wasn't doing anything to help Kate, when they both knew she could somehow, but because she kept seeing those images in her head- over and over. She didn't believe Julie when she'd said they weren't real. *They can't just be worst-case-scenario images.* Sadie thought, *if they were, why do they keep changing and why can I feel the pain that Kate is feeling?*

"Julie, you need to do something." Sadie said loud enough so her sister could hear from the other room.

"I told you what Kate said. We can't go until three o'clock. If we show up before that, who ever is holding her captive will get mad. We don't know who or what they are, therefore we don't want to make them angry." Julie was now standing in Sadie's bedroom doorway.

"Do another spell. Make it so we can see her. That way I can get these images out of my head."

"I do know of one demonette we can call to help us. But this could go very wrong, Sadie. I'm not that powerful when it comes to controlling demonettes. Even a witch as powerful as me doesn't easily control them. And they were made by The Devil, we don't want to mess with him." demonettes are goddesses that don't have a soul. They are higher than the human with no soul, or demon, but they are still lower than goddesses on the scale of power. Usually a witch would call upon a demonette because they need help undoing an evil act or event or the demonette is needed to perform the evil act or event. Shea is the demonette of visions. She is one of the less evil demonettes that Julie dared to call upon for help. By bringing the demonette of visions, Shea could tell the caller exactly where to find who or what they were looking for or just a general area. Shea was one of the few *trustworthy* demonettes. Also as the demonette of visions, Shea could tell a person or witch what their future holds for them, but Shea doesn't enjoy ruining the surprise of the future so she tries to say no to that sort of call.

"Julie. It's like our only choice. If you really think we should just sit here and do diddly-squat, then you don't love Kate as the sister she is. You have power, more power than you give yourself credit for. Just do it." Sadie ranted.

"Alright. I agree that just sitting here isn't going to help Kate. But you have to understand that I'm not strong enough to both bring forth Shea and control her. She is of her own free will once she's here. And if that goes wrong, she will cause more mayhem than any of us would like. I guess we can try. If it goes wrong, we should be prepared to do the undo charm. I need my white and my green candle. We'll try just calling her for help before trying to summon her to form." Calling upon a demonette is not at all the same as summoning them. Calling on them for help is the not physical way of getting help from them. Usually they will only tell the witch how to help themselves in the situation. But summoning is bringing forth the demonette to form physically in front of the witch that did the summoning. By summoning a demonette, Julie is asking for the help to be taken care of by the demonette; by summoning, the demonette does all the work after they agree that the witch is in need of their help. But if the demonette does not believe that the witch who summoned them needs their help, the demonette is not obligated to go away. They can stay around on Earth and go do their own business; causing destruction and mayhem if so desired.

Sadie ran to the supplies room and got a new white candle and a new green candle. The lighter was already in front of Julie.

"For this one, Sadie, all I need you to do is stop any bleeding, and keep me from falling. You might want to grab some towels." Julie suggested.

"Bleeding? Like nose bleeds?" this was a usual side effect of performing a spell; and the girls knew that all too well.

"More than the usual." Julie said, mentally asking Sadie if she really had to do this. It wasn't her favorite part of being a witch- calling on demonettes. Especially because they knew exactly where Kate was- In the bar called Mixed. Julie was doing this more for the benefit of a calm Sadie. Julie set the green candle on her left and the white one in front of it and a little to the right so it was in front of her knee, "Shea. demonette of visions. demonette of the future. demonette of the light beyond the darkness. Hear my call. I call on thee to give me the power. Give me the power to see my sister. Kate is away and I wish to see her. Shea. You are the demonette of visions. Give me your vision." Nothing was working. Julie kept repeating the words she'd spoken and nothing happened. Sadie was waiting for blood to come pouring out of Julie's nose or ears or eyes because those were the usual places; but there was nothing.

"Julie, I don't think it's working." Sadie finally said.

"I agree. Do you want me to try summoning her?"

"It's almost three, so let's just go to the bar, blend in and then at three, make our move." Sadie suggested.

"Agreed."

— — —

Kate felt like today was the day that her sisters were finally going to come find her. There was a surge that went through her body that told her Julie and Sadie were coming. *Today's the day. Sadie and Julie are going to come find me. One problem on hand. I don't know that I want to leave. It's not like Tyson is violent and he's sweet when he wants to be. I think he could, actually, help us out a lot. Maybe I can still be around him but leave with my sisters too.* Kate thought, *maybe I can convince Julie and Sadie that Tyson has information that he won't give us unless we let him join us. Even though that's not true.* Tyson came back down stairs and saw that Kate and one of the guards were playing a card game. Kate was now wearing her leather outfit again and in her mind she was trying to think of a way to convince her sisters that they needed Tyson.

"Hey Tyson. Want to play?" Kate asked casually. She was acting like she wasn't his captive anymore, which was more or less true. Tyson told Kate she could leave anytime she wanted; she just wasn't taking him up on that offer.

"No. What I want is for my workers to go upstairs and start making drinks."

"It's not my shift. I don't know why you're getting all hostile about it. Technically I don't work here anymore. Unless you are going to pay me the normal pay for a waitress that's forced to wear a too-tight uniform…" Kate started to suggest.

"No. I'm not going to pay you. But you're right, you don't work here and you aren't forced to be here anymore. Why are you still here? I have gotten everything I needed from you."

Something is clearly up. I told Kate yesterday that she was free to go because I have no more questions for her or a reason to keep her here; but she's still here! I kind of like that she didn't scurry to get out of here as soon as I let her go. But I also feel like she has a reason *to stay and now I want to know what the reason is.* Tyson thought, *and I want to know does she plan on staying here for a while?*

"I want to convince my sisters, when they show up, that you should join us. You may have everything you need from me but I have yet to get more than half of my questions answered. According to Gust, you are the only vampire in existence that would know anything I want to know about The Devil." *Oh!* Tyson thought with a little happy in his surprised expression, *that works perfectly. I can tag along with them and gain their trust so I can lure them into my boss's trap.*

"Fair enough. I'll join if they invite me to." Tyson smiled. *Maybe, somehow, this was his plan all along. Maybe I do want to leave, but he's still making me stay. Otherwise wouldn't he argue more about joining the forces of good with my sisters and me?* Kate became suspicious.

— — —

"Julie, we need to go. Now!" Sadie yelled. Sadie was now getting an unusual tap into Kate's emotions, "I think she's fallen for him." Somehow Sadie could read Kate's mind even from this far away. Every once in a while, Sadie would get little glimpses of magic being unknowingly used by her. Sadie figured out that these times of her randomly using the simplest spells were due to her always helping Julie with her magic. She was now just so used to it that she didn't even think twice when it happened.

This time was different, though. This time, she had apparently used a very complicated and advanced spell to tap into Kate's emotions. Julie wasn't even a master at this spell yet and she'd been going at it for almost a whole year.

"No way. Kate wouldn't do that. She's smart. But we should go. It's nearly three." Julie agreed and they were on their way to the car, "If we drive, he'll be able to follow us back."

"How else are we supposed to get there?" Sadie asked and then caught onto the idea of magic, "What supplies do you need?"

"I don't need any supplies. I just need the power that I have already in me." It was silent for about a minute while Julie silently called upon the goddess of the Earth. Jade came through with granting the wish to teleport the two girls from their home to their destination. But she forewarned Julie that only one would have that same way back home. The others would have to find their own way. Jade was an exception to the process of becoming a goddess. She was changed into a vampire by force and immediately after the change was complete, Jade sacrificed herself to save her maker's life. God, himself, saw this as an act of forgiveness and decided to upgrade Jade to be a goddess. She is the only known goddess that has no soul. She is also the only known goddess that can teleport people through thought and because of this, all Julie had to do was call upon her in order to be teleported along with Sadie to where Kate was- no summoning was needed when usually it would be.

Julie and Sadie walked into the bar, not at all dressed appropriately. They were in fighting clothes, not sexy on-the-job clothes like Kate had been. Julie felt a force of evil come across her as soon as she laid eyes on Tyson behind the bar. She knew exactly who that was and she knew this was the place. Somehow, she knew he was Kate's captor.

"Sadie, I'll meet you at that table. I'm going to go get our drinks." Julie claimed. Sadie nodded and headed towards the table Julie had pointed at after being told what kind of drink her sister wanted. Instead of getting the drinks though, Julie had another plan up her sleeve. She went straight for Tyson. Tyson, of course, had no idea who she was. He only knew she looked like Kate and therefore she must be a 666 girl. *Oh God! She's going to cause a huge scene, I can just tell. Just play cool, Ty, it's not like you really still have their sister held against her will. She's here by choice*

now, and that means you have nothing to hide.
Where's the other girl? Here she comes.

"Hello pretty lady. Would you like a drink?" he asked. Julie just smiled and nodded.

"I'll have a Cosmo." Tyson knew those words. They had come out of Kate's mouth the night they'd met about a week ago.

"What's a small town girl like you doing in a bar like this?" Julie noticed his nametag. *Perfect.* She thought. His nametag said Tyson. *This is definitely him. I got him Kate; we're coming to get you out of there.*

"Actually, Tyson, I came here for a specific reason. I want to know if you have seen my sister around here. She's about this high, and looks, oh I don't know, exactly like me? Before you answer though Tyson, I feel it is necessary to inform you that I already know the answer. You have my sister somewhere locked up and kept against her will. I know this because she told me. My name is Julie, by the way. Julie Sanders."

"So I *was* correct. You are Kate's sister; you are a 666 girl. And if I'm not mistaken, you must be the really powerful witch, Kate was telling me about. Nope. Haven't seen her."

"Seriously? You are going to do this? Okay. Have it your way." Julie walked off and over to the table Sadie was sitting at.

"Where are our drinks?"

"Oh. Sorry, the bartender kind of pissed me off. But I know where Kate is."

"Does the bartender have her somewhere?"

"I believe so. And he knows I'm a witch. Since he's up here and not by Kate, I'm going to do a locater spell so we can be sure. If Kate is here, we should be ready to fight. And I know just how to fight him off if we need to." Julie stated. "Sadie, can you do me a favor while I do the locater spell?" Sadie nodded, "Threaten the bar."

"What? Why?"

"Please? Otherwise he's going to see the smoke and know something is up."

Chapter 5

"Noah. God of People. I call on thee to help me locate my sister." Julie started the locater spell while Sadie tried to think of how to threaten the whole bar. Sadie got up on a table nearby and called out for everyone's attention. Being the god of people does not mean that Noah is the god of all. Nope! God of people simply means that Noah has the power to locate lost and missing people. The only spell that Noah is called upon for is the locator spell; and the locator spell is only used when one is desperate to find a missing person or being. Noah is always willing to help find the missing.

"My sister has gone missing. She looks exactly like me but with red hair. If anyone here knows she's here or knows where she is, I need you to speak up. I need to find her today. I swear to you, I have a bomb in this bar and as we speak it is ticking lower and lower." Sadie lied, "I will disarm it if someone speaks up. Speak up!" *Lame, Sadie, lame! I can't believe I can't threaten a stupid club, or distract everyone from what Julie is doing. Do it better!* Sadie cheered herself on; but she didn't continue.

"Sadie, is it?" Tyson walked up to the table Sadie was standing on.

"That doesn't matter. Do you know where my sister is?" Sadie demanded.

"I might. But what is your witch-sister doing?" Tyson asked looking over in Julie's direction. To perform a locator spell, Julie has to call upon Noah. He's always waiting around to help out and find a missing person but Julie has to be careful about where she performs the locator spell. It's a spell that creates obvious looking smoke and fumes while Julie basically has to yell out the words of the spell. On the sending end, there is smoke of several colors starting at pink and going to blue. This made casting the spell in public obvious. On the receiving end, the locator is an eye ball looking around an area that the lost person is in. The eye doesn't necessarily see the lost person but it sees the surroundings of them. It's also very important to be careful of when Julie performs the spell because the eye ball floating in mid air and looking around is obvious to the people that are in the surroundings of the lost or missing being. If she's not careful, the captor could see the eye and if they are smart, they'll know what that means and trace the spell back to her.

Julie looked up to see Tyson coming straight for her. She was done with her spell and stood from her stool. Tyson stopped about three feet from her.

"Do you really have a bomb in my bar?" Tyson asked Julie.

"That depends." Julie answered with a smile, "Do you know where our sister is? I just preformed a locater spell. I know she's nearby in some sort of basement or office. You are going to take us to her."

"How about we make something clear. You are not the boss of me. I'm the one that has your sister, you are the ones that are going to listen." Julie used her telekinetic power to pick up the stool she just stood from and brought it to her hands. Julie didn't usually use her telekinetic power unless she needs to show off her power to scare someone. It was a very simple silent spell that could be performed by thinking about an object coming to her without being moved by physical touch.

"Tyson, I have the feeling, deep in my gut, that if you don't take us to our sister right *now,* you will regret that decision. You don't understand how powerful a witch can be until you've seen what *I* can do. I could go to the dark side if I wanted to because of how much power I have in me. Do you really want to test your luck?" Julie started, "None of your customers are going to come back after I'm through with this place if you don't take us to her." Julie threatened. Following her threatening statement, Julie smashed the stool in her hand to the ground. As a result there was a dent in the dance floor and a broken wood bar stool's scattered pieces all around Tyson and Julie's feet.

"Alright, alright. She's in the basement. I swear to you, though, I told her three days ago that she could go home. She is the one who wanted to stay here. Follow me." This was only a slight lie. Tyson told Kate one day ago that Kate could leave, not three. Tyson led the girls to the basement where Kate was playing another game of cards with the guards.

As they walked down the flight of stairs, Sadie commented, "If that were true, she would have called. And she wouldn't have told us she was in danger."

"I don't understand what that means, since there's no way she could have talked to you while being here, she is free to go as of three days ago. Talk to her about why she never called or left." Tyson exclaimed.

"Oh hey, sisters! What the *hell* are you doing here?" Kate said with excitement.

"What are *we* doing here? We are saving *your* ass!" Sadie said with anger ripping through her calm voice. Everyone could tell she was angry but she was trying to hide it.

"Why the anger sis? What's wrong with you?" Kate asked as though nothing was up.

"What is wrong with me is it looks like you've been comfortably living here with the vampire that took you against your will for a couple of days now. And you are playing fucking cards! With! The! Guards! You didn't even think to call! How dare you put us through nights of sleeplessness! How dare you put Julie through dangerous spells and summonsing! We did countless spells to find out where the hell you were and you even told us, yourself, that you were in danger. To worry your sisters like that as a joke, that's just immoral. Are you even our sister?"

"What! What are you talking about! I never told you that I was in danger. I didn't call because they took my cell phone and I couldn't get through to Julie in my thoughts. Of course I'm your sister! Honestly I stayed here because I needed more information from Tyson. I think he could be a lot of use to us. I'm sorry you lost sleep and I'm sorry for worrying you so much but I legitimately was just doing my job! And what do you mean you did spells and summonsing? Who did you summon? What do you mean by I told you I was in danger? How did I do that without knowing I did? What is going on?"

"It was probably the magic going wrong." Tyson suggested, "Or maybe a friend of whom ever you summoned was just trying to teach you to be careful by faking contact with your sister."

"I didn't do any magic that time. The force contacted *me*. I don't know of any demonettes or goddesses that could fake contact from my sister. And who are you to tell me I'm a bad witch!"

"Whoa! I *never* said you were a bad witch, Julie.

I just suggested that maybe, somehow you did cause that magic without knowing so and you believed it was Kate. There are things a witch such as you can do without using a spell or summoning charm. You could have just wished that Kate would contact you through that thought thing and tell you where she was. And then you thought it was her when it actually happened." Tyson made a point, "I am not saying that you are a bad witch. I'm saying quite the opposite. Maybe you are powerful enough of a witch to make things happen just by thinking about them. Which would be very impressive."

"You are a vampire. How would you know anything about magic or witches?"

"I may be just a vampire, Julie, but I am a vampire that has been around for centuries. You wouldn't believe me if I told you how many witches I've come across. They are more common than you think. Even *they* could do that type of thing, and they were not even close to your potential of power. But I can clearly see that I have crossed a line here, and I will now be going back up to my business." Tyson finished and turned around to walk up the steps.

"Tyson, wait. My sisters might not see it right now, but I *know* you can help us find Sage. The fact that one of my most reliable contacts sent me to you for the information is one amazing piece of proof. I think, even if Julie and Sadie are not on board yet, I think you should come with us and help us. You told me that you wanted to start doing good…"

"Kate. That's sweet. But I can do good in other ways too. I'll stick to my statement earlier. I will come with if they concur." Tyson walked up the rest of the steps and Kate turned to her sisters.

"Julie, I know you don't like vampires. Who am I to say they are good creatures, I just got kidnapped by one. But Tyson is important to our process. I can feel it. I just somehow know that he is the only one that can give us information about Sage."

"Who's Sage?" Sadie asked.

"The demon that we are after, with over six hundred collected souls. First of all, his name is Sage but I also have some important facts. He's The Devil. He's coming after us. And Tyson knows everything there is to know about him." Kate answered.

"How?" Julie asked.

"Ask him. I don't know." Kate commented.

Sadie, Julie and Kate all walked up to the club

part of the building. Tyson was taking an order from a customer while other customers were telling him to hurry up. Kate offered to help.

"Do I have to pay you?" Tyson asked, "I don't have the money for another employee."

"Give me twenty bucks plus I keep my tips and we'll call it even." Kate suggested.

"Fine. Thanks."

"Kate, you're working with him now?" Julie asked, astounded. *How dare Kate! Working with a vampire? Not just that, oh no! A vampire that held her against her will in his basement! She's working with him! What has gotten into her? I think Sadie might have been right; I think Kate has fallen for Tyson.*

"He needs help. If I help him, he may decide to help us."

"We don't *need* his help." Sadie vigorously told Kate, "Kate. You are helping the enemy. This is the guy that held you against your will for days with no contact with your sisters allowed."

"This is also the guy that gave us the information that I just told you. Like the fact that we are after the freaking…" she lowered her voice, "Devil. We know how old he is in Devil years; we know what his collection number is. We know a lot of things that we didn't know before all because of Tyson. So if you think for one second that you are going to convince me that he can't help us, you are wrong. Completely wrong! He is basically our only chance in succeeding." *Oh yeah. I do think we can beat Sage. No doubt. We just need Tyson. Honestly I think the main reason I want Tyson with us is so that I can get to know him a little better. I want to learn more about his past, how he became a vampire and stuff like that. But I also very much believe that we need him, his knowledge and his guidance. I believe that we need his help for a lot of things, only one of which is to defeat Sage. So, yeah, I trust that we can win against Sage, The Devil, but we need Tyson; I can just feel it.*

"Okay. So we let him help us. What then?"

"What do you mean what then? He helps us, we go in for the kill and then all evil things on the planet disappear." Kate said. She was getting aggravated with her sisters. They wouldn't listen to her. Kate thought she was making perfectly good sense but all Sadie and Julie were hearing was 'I'm the boss, I'm in charge, you will listen to what I have to say and do what I think is necessary'.

"Girls. If you are going to argue about this, please take it down stairs." Tyson said calmly, helping another customer. *Okay, so I kind of want to help them; like seriously help them. But that's only because I'm sick of being Sage's pet. I mean come on! Sage isn't even the real Devil. These girls don't know that. And I'm not supposed to know that but I overheard Sage talking to his 'boss' so I am thinking that means he's not at the top of the line of evil beings. So I kind of want to help them because I kind of want to defeat Sage. But at the same time, I don't want to help them because I know Sage will eventually find out and that could just go badly. Super badly.*

"Oh, you would like that, wouldn't you? Then you may as well lock the door behind us, right? Keep *us* here too? Against our will just like you did with Kate."

"Sadie! Would you stop! Tyson only kept me down there against my will for two days. The other three were by my choice. You don't have the right to blame him for keeping me here. I wanted to be here." Kate yelled at her sister.

"Here's the deal Kate. Tyson can tag along for a while. You obviously, for some insane reason, trust him or something. If he proves to be useful, he can join us. But he has to prove himself first, before *we* trust him. Got it?" Julie said loud enough for Tyson to hear. He smiled at Kate and then at the other girls. *I think I would have tagged along even if they said no to the idea, secretly. And I think, secretly, Sadie and Julie both know deep down that their sister is right when she says that they need me. Not only for information, but for strength and strategy too. They almost have completely nothing without me.*

Then Tyson announced to the customers that the bar was closing early. Due to 'personal happenings'.

"Why'd you do that?" Kate asked.

"So we can talk privately without me being accused of kidnapping." Tyson said with an annoyed tone towards Sadie, the one that had accused him of such.

"To be fair, you *did* kidnap me." Kate commented.

"Yes, well, I assure you it won't happen again. Since now I won't have to in order to get information from you." Tyson said with a wide smile.

— — —

"What is wrong with you, Sadie?" Kate asked.

"I don't like that you are making us work with a vampire. It's not smart. And it's not right."

It's not that I don't like vampires, I do…actually that's a lie, I don't. But I have a good reason. That reason is that I don't like having to go out and kill all these vampires and other types of demons because they are all evil. I don't really understand why this Sage guy had to go and make all of these demons. I guess in a way, I should be blaming my ancestors. They *are the ones that trapped Sage in his own Hell Dimension with that stupid curse to lock him in there in the first place.* Sadie thought, *But then again, what would the world be like with Sage free?*

"Soon enough Sadie, I have a feeling, you will not see me as a vampire anymore. I'll just be another person helping you. You know not all of us vampires are evil…" Tyson started, "Let me prove I'm one of the good ones…" Tyson gave Sadie a wide 'give me a chance' smile.

"You have a lot to prove before I'll believe that."

"The real thing that we need to be focusing on

right now is will you give me a chance to prove what I need to prove? Or are you going to stay closed minded about vampires."

"No, Tyson, the real thing that we need to focus on is Sage, and how to kill him."

"You do know that killing The Devil is going to kill all evil things on the planet and in the universe, right?" Tyson argued with raised eyebrows and wide eyes. Julie has her ways of being a witch and secretly finding out information without even her sisters knowing. She, in her mind, did research on Sage starting as soon as she learned that Sage was The Devil.

"Yes we know this. That isn't our biggest concern right now though." Julie said.

The four of them were in the Sanders' living room around the coffee table. Tyson and Kate were sitting on the couch while Julie and Sadie each were in a chair. There was a notebook in front of Kate for taking notes on what Tyson knew about the victim demon.

"Of course it isn't. Because you girls are all about saving the world." Tyson said as he grew more and more annoyed.

"That's us." Julie smiled.

"You know the evil in the world doesn't only include demons. And the good doesn't only include humans." Tyson informed the girls. "You would be keeping some demons and murdering some humans. You will end up messing up the balance of good and evil if you kill The Devil. Either that or you will just create another Devil that could be worse than our current one. There is more that I need to tell you".

— — —

I like Sadie because she's down to earth but she's determined. She will do anything to save the world; even if it came down to sacrificing her own family. Normally, a human girl at that age would be more like Kate: protecting of the family and loved ones. Kate is down to earth but what I like about Sadie is that she will literally do anything to save the humans she doesn't know even over her own life and her family's lives. She is caring but if it were ever to come down to a choice between saving her family and saving a billion strangers, she'd pick the strangers any day. I like that because it shows strength. Who else on this planet would be strong enough to say goodbye to her family in order to make humanity continue. Tyson thought to himself. *I just wish she would like me back. Or at least show interest in learning more about vampires.*

I don't think I'm in love with her, no, because I can't be in love with her and her sister Kate. And I know I'm in love with Kate. Kate is down to earth and will sacrifice a billion plus strangers over losing her family. This is amazing because she would never give up her family even for a second if she had a choice between saving them and the rest of the human race. She is also very amazing, in my eyes, because she is open minded to the topic of vampires. She thinks we are amazingly interesting creatures and keeps asking me questions like how to be turned and stuff. I think it is really cool that a human is so curious about vampires and the vampire history. I love Kate. I thought at first it was just as a friend but I've grown on her and she's grown on me. Quickly but still fully. I really like her personality, she's really beautiful and I love the protectiveness of her family and the leadership role she has on the 666 group. I love everything about her.

Chapter 6

Tyson

"You know I can help you but I'm not going to answer your questions until you answer mine, girls. Kate already has kind of answered these questions."

"Tyson, I don't like this. Don't do that to them." Kate told me.

"Do what?" I asked with a slight smile. The truth was that I knew exactly what Kate was referring to.

Kate had been held against her will by me for only three days. She, now, was referring to the dramatic attitude change in those three days. I went from nice and friendly to rude. I guess I just don't really understand the reason as to why she didn't want me to ask Julie and Sadie questions. I mean, Julie is a witch. She could know things.

"You know exactly what I'm talking about. You got all friendly with me and then it was suddenly interrogation time. Don't do that again. Just answer their questions, please." Kate told me.

Kate was like that; always up in my face with rules and restrictions. I knew that I was supposed to be helping *them* find Sage but I felt bad that there was no possible way they would ever beat Sage in a fight. Even with the most powerful witch on earth. I was changed and raised by the man and that means I know his deepest and darkest secrets and I know all of his strengths and all of his weaknesses.

"How do you know so much about Sage?" Sadie asked.

"Hello? Vampire? All vampires know about The Devil. How can we not? He's the reason we exist!" Tyson said.

"I don't believe that. Not every vampire, ghoul and were-person can exist *only* because Sage is The Devil. What about before Sage?" Kate asked. Wow, I guess she's smarter than she seems.

"What do you mean before Sage? Kate, there has always been a Devil. Meaning Sage has always been The Devil." Julie insisted.

While the girls were arguing over something I was soon going to reveal the truth about, I glanced at each of them out of curiosity to see which one seemed the most likely to go for a vampire like myself. Kate so far was the only one of the three that didn't need any convincing that vampires and other demon types could possibly be not-evil but I guess you'll never know how you can convince someone unless you've tried.

So after I read each girl more than I have ever read a girl in my long after-life, I came to the conclusion that if I was going to choose either Julie or Sadie, it would have to be Julie because she and I had something in common. And that was, we were both technically, not human. She's a witch, which according to the past that meant she isn't human. And I am a vampire. A human with his soul taken from him not by choice. That is when I realized that Julie was asking me a question.

"So *how* do you know everything about Sage? Other than the fact that you claim all demons exist only because of Sage, how do you know like every fact about him?"

"I know him personally." Sage and I weren't friends, actually. We were of different ages and frankly, Sage wanted nothing to do with a kid like me. Until I became part of his "Home." His "Home" was where he kept the children of the families he had his workers kill. There were at most up to twenty-five of us and every time someone would turn seventeen, they would become part of the drawing. The drawing was a so-called competition to see if you would be the next to be "Chosen." And to be "Chosen" was to be made a horrible deal. "A Deal with Sage" was a deal with The Devil. Every time someone got brought to Sage to have this deal be made with them, they would only get two choices. Die, or live as the undead. Either way, the kid's *soul* was taken from them to add to the count of six hundred and sixty six souls that Sage had to collect. All of us kids were helping set The Devil free onto Earth.

"You are *friends* with The Devil and you wait until *now* to tell us this?" Kate barked at me. I looked at her with a confused expression, "Tyson, you just claimed that you personally know The Devil. Unless you are now claiming to be his friend, you are going to have to explain this statement a little more." We hate each other- Sage and I. There isn't one person on this planet that I hate more than I hate my maker. Sage forced me to choose death or walking death; that isn't the greatest of choices if you ask me. The relationship between us isn't even a relationship because it's just horrible.

"I was friends with him back when he was a non-magic user. We were both humans." I lied.

"Who made you into a vampire?" Sadie asked suspiciously.

"I don't remember. I only remember seeing a familiar face and then a bloody neck after I woke up." I said, lying once again.

"A familiar face? So you were made by Sage?"

"No. I don't know who made me." I lied, "I mean Evil beings exist because The Devil exists. If he's not alive, then we all die cold turkey." There I go lying again, "I am a vampire. Vampires are made out to be evil things and only individually can we change that. I don't think it's a fair statement to claim that I was made by such a beast. Also, something I'm convinced you will have a hard time believing is that The Devil is not a demon."

"What do you mean? Is he a ghost? Spirit?" Kate was the most shocked at this. I knew it was going to take them a while to understand this part of the information but I also knew that at one point I would have to explain it. May as well get it over with, right? Why is Julie not surprised that Sage is human? Did she already know this and not tell her sisters? That doesn't seem like her, from what I know about her...

"No. I mean, he's not a demon; he's a human being. It doesn't surprise me that you didn't know this but you would think some time in the past they would have passed this information on from one generation to the next." I told the girls. This is how I see the history of these three girls. They are the thirteenth generation of the Sanders' girls and they are not the reason for Sage being trapped in his own Hell dimension- their ancestors are. The first generation of the 666 group became the 666 group by putting Sage in Hell and trapped him there with a curse. The only problem was they did *not* think their curse through before putting it on Sage with only one way out. Back then, they weren't really all that smart when coming up with things and making big decisions.

Sadie had the hardest time understanding the concept of The Devil being human, "What are you talking about? He can't be a human being. Humans are not capable of that kind of thing. This isn't possible. You're lying. You have to be." I guess the thought of a human being, taking over six hundred souls of other human beings, kind of frightened her a little.

Sadie is a kind girl. She has perfect skin and pearly blond hair that surrounds her perfect looking face. Kate and Sadie look a lot alike other than their hair color. The three of them have different hair color but that's the only thing that makes them different from each other. Sadie is smarter than Julie and Kate, Kate is more of an extrovert, and Julie is more of the quiet type in the corner reading books but they are all the same on the outside.

"There's something I have to tell you about your family history." I stated.

Chapter 7

"Okay so what's this about our family history? How do you know about it?" Julie asked Tyson as they all sat on the couch and chair that surrounded their coffee table. The front entry of the house led straight through the long hallway. Along the hallway were three doors leading to the living room, Kate's bedroom and the witch closet. Each of the girls had their own bedroom and their own office. There were two witch closets in the house, one on the main level across from the living room and one next to Julie's bedroom. The only way to get to Kate's office is to go through her bedroom and to have a key that opens the lock; a copy of this key went to Sadie and Julie and Kate. Kate's bedroom and office were on the main level while Sadie and Julie lived upstairs. The stairs that led up to the top level of the Sanders' home was a spiral staircase.

"The Sanders family is known to have three girl names used throughout it's history. Kate; the leader of each set of triplets. Sadie; the fighter and warrior of the group that will stop at nothing to save the world. Julie; the witch of the family that is more powerful in every generation. Back in the 1800s Kate, Sadie and Julie Sanders were the first generation of the set of triplets named this. The girls came up against demons, vampires, spirits, and the human demons. But there was one in particular that had a past of black magic. He was a human being and his name was Sage Simmons He loved using magic for everything. If the remote was too far for him to reach, he'd use magic to get it for him. If he wanted to have sex with some cute girl, he'd put a spell on her to make her agree. So on and so forth. You get the point." The girls stared at Tyson as he continued. He couldn't really tell if they were believing him or not.

"After a while that magic use became an obsession to become more powerful than anyone had ever heard of. Before this time, Hell did not exist. Not technically I mean. Actually, Sage was the creator of the Hell that we know of. He became so powerful that he could make a whole part of the world underneath the core of our Earth. Really what Sage did was rip a part of the universe's atmosphere and created another part of the earth underneath the core; he expanded the Earth a little. Some people believe otherwise but this is what I know and go by. But I do know of another guy that claims to also be The Devil.

"By this time, Sage's magic obsession was made public and he was known for the black magic. Also by this time, Kate and Sadie and Julie were known for fighting off others that were almost as bad as Sage. They weren't as well known to the demons around them as you three are today but they were still not only shadows either. They were strong in comparison to the demons that followed Sage's example. You have to remember that all of these demons that followed Sage were just human beings. Human beings with magic as their addicting and murderous drug. The Sanders girls didn't care, they killed these so called demons anyway because they were using the magic to rob stores and banks and to do other bad deeds. Your ancestors were true murderers. They didn't stop at humans; they killed all that completed a bad deed towards another." Tyson paused. For a second, Tyson thought that Sadie or Kate was going to say something about all of this information. Once he saw that their open mouths were just a reaction to the history of their family, Tyson continued once again.

"But when it came to Sage, they couldn't find a way to kill him. He was too strong. He was so strong that he put Sadie in a trance of sleep. Such deep sleep that she was dying day by day because she couldn't wake up. So instead of just plain killing Sage, Julie put a curse on him that could only be broken in one way.

"Sage's obsession for power overthrew his control on the power that he already had in his system. He created Hell and the Sanders girls' curse started with trapping him down there. The unbreakable gateway to Hell could only be, and still can only be, opened if Sage collects six hundred and sixty six souls. But there's a catch. One of those souls has to be a Sander's soul." Tyson explained to the girls.

"Wait. What do you mean by collecting souls? Like...killing people?"

"No. I mean turning innocent human beings into demons. Technically he didn't have to turn to that, he could have just killed them but that would mean that he was a murderer and Sage thought that having the decency of not killing innocent people made him more…civil. Killing someone is the same as stealing their soul from them. But killing someone and ridding them of their soul *and* bringing them back as the undead to live on with their lives, that's what Sage decided to do; in a way it was to make his own army of soulless creatures. So he decided to kill the innocent men and women and kids and bring them back as demons. It didn't matter what breed of demon that he turned them into as long as the soul was collected. Could have been the vampire breed, the spirit breed or the were-breed. He mixed it up a little. Any demon that you've come across and killed, Sage most likely had made that human being into that creature. Don't get me wrong, you Sanders girls are doing the right thing by ridding this world of those monsters but if you think about it technically, you three girls are murderers just like your ancestors." Tyson joked. He laughed and then looked at the three girls' expressions. They either didn't get the joke or they didn't think it was funny, so Tyson moved on, "Anyway, there is also another catch. The souls that Sage collects have to be pure souls. They have to be noble and good. Not of those that followed him previously. According to your ancestors Kate, Julie and Sadie, those people that followed Sage around like dogs, were already soulless.

And by the way, Kate, you were right when you said you are not caught up with your research on his kill streak. He has collected six hundred and forty four souls so far and only has twenty-two to go. And one of you three has to be the last one."

"What would happen if that comes true? Would he be freed? What would happen?" Julie asked. *What would have happened if our ancestors never trapped Sage in Hell? Would Sage be dead by now because he's only human or would there already be Hell on Earth because no one did anything about him? Or would he have gotten bored with his magic and just stopped? Putting that to the side, though, what will happen now…if Sage were to be freed? Obviously we would have our work cut out for us but would he come after Kate, Sadie and me? Would he make us pay for what our ancestors did to him? According to Tyson, one of us would have to be dead or turned over for him to be set free, so would he come after us even after making one of us one of his creations?* Julie's thoughts raced with all of these questions and more, making her crazy with worry.

"That doesn't matter, because we aren't going to let it happen. Okay? The three of us are staying human beings and that's not going to change. Tyson, I don't understand how you could know all this. Are you like working for him or something?" *Shit! Am I being obvious? Did I tell them too much?* Tyson thought to himself but, to the girls, he just shook his head and looked normal, "Then how do you know about the history of our family? How do you know more than we know?"

"Because I actually cared about who I was up against. I did my research on you while you were my captive, Kate. I read your body language and I read books and journals about the Sanders family. Your ancestors had the right idea, keeping journals about their adventures."

"What generation are we of the Sanders' demon hunters? I mean, I knew our family had a past of doing this and I knew that our names were used throughout the history of our family but what generation are we?" Kate questioned. *Tyson said that generation one of us Sanders girls put and trapped Sage in his own Hell dimension. We didn't really know anything about our past until he informed us so I think we have to be at least a little ways into the future of the first generation. Like maybe generation ten or eleven. Maybe?* Kate calculated.

"I believe you are the thirteenth generation." Tyson answered honestly, "You might be the fourteenth, though. Not a hundred percent sure. Why does it matter?"

"Well you said that Julie gets stronger and stronger from generation to generation. I was just curious for her sake, I guess." Kate commented glancing over at Julie. Julie looked at Kate as though she was happy with the decision to let Tyson into the group. Though it had messed with their reputation as no-mercy demon hunters, Tyson had been a great deal of help so far. And she didn't think that was going to change any time soon. But maybe she was wrong.

Julie and Sadie both had a gut feeling that something fishy was going on with Tyson. He kept talking about Sage like he was made to work for him. Made by Sage, to work for Sage. Honestly, it wouldn't surprise Julie if this was true but at the same time, she wasn't sure that was the fishy feeling she and her sister had. Maybe it just had to do with Kate's love for the vampire that kept her prisoner or a vampire in general. Julie, for one, was not the biggest fan of that. *I hate vampires. I hate all of the many kinds of demons but especially vampires.* Julie thought. *This is not an irrational hate though, my hate for vampires started when Tyson came into our lives. This is probably the less than rational part of my hate: I don't like the vampire race as a whole because Kate, of all people, is falling for who could be the one vampire working for Sage. He refuses to tell us who his maker is and I have a feeling, a very strong feeling, that Tyson is hiding something big from us. I just don't want Kate to find out the hard way and get her heart broken …again…and this time by someone that isn't even alive!*

"I did say that but from what I can tell, you, Julie, are the most powerful anyone has ever seen a witch become. Even being the thirteenth or fourteenth generation of very powerful witches, you are far more advanced than only the thirteenth generation. You are more like the thirtieth generation if you want to speak by power. You should be careful with the power that you have, though."

"Why?" Julie asked Tyson after becoming excited that she was more powerful than her generation number would ever have predicted. *This is so cool! But…calm down Julie… it's a vampire telling you all of this. Probably only to get on your good side. Calm down. He's probably just making the whole thing up.* Trying to convince herself of this was not going to work because Julie was indeed excited about being more powerful than the generation number of thirteen generations in the family would have predicted.

"Because Sage was almost as powerful as you when he turned to the dark side. Don't get to the point of …just make sure you can control the magic in you before you go destroy the world. Wouldn't want you to become the next Devil if you girls ever end up killing the one we've got now. That lifestyle sucks."

I can just see how this is going to go. Julie is going to make being more powerful than predicted go straight to her head. I think it's great if it's actually true that she's more powerful than the ancestry of our family predicted but I don't want her to mess up just because she's being cocky about her power. Hopefully this won't happen. All we can do is hope. Kate contemplated. *And how does Tyson know so much? About vampires, about Sage and about our family? Why didn't he tell me this earlier? Maybe Sadie and Julie were right. Maybe I shouldn't trust Tyson so quickly. Maybe he is secretly working with or even for Sage. I mean he won't even tell us the name of the vampire that changed him. I personally don't think that should be considered a personal item of information to not be shared. And we barely know anything about him other than he's a really old vampire with a lot of connections and a lot of information. He can't even give a straight answer on how he knows what he knows.*

"How would you know?" Kate was getting more suspicious now.

Chapter 8

Tyson

I wonder what would happen if I just quit working for him. Sage and I had an agreement but he never really told me what would happen if I broke my half of it. Would I die? Would that be the best thing? I know for a fact that these girls won't be able to kill him alone. Even with me by their sides, it'll be a hard task. Do I want to kill him? I love being a vampire. Though I hate hurting people just to survive, I still love being immortal and seeing all the changes in society. It's amazing how things have changed. What the girls don't know, other than the fact that I work for Sage, is that I met their ancestors. I was their prisoner for a whole year until I proved to be useful. This was after I was turned into a vampire.

I was turned on my seventeenth birthday though I look like I'm about today's version of thirty. Sage came up to me and offered me a deal. He told me that I had a choice between dying right there or I could join him. I asked him what joining him would mean. He never really gave me a straight answer now that I think about it; he just told me I would like it better than true death. I never thought about his word choice. He mentioned true death as though it were a different thing then just death. But back then, honestly, becoming a vampire was almost like just becoming a real adult; another part of life. And I was taught to believe that it was just another part of life that everyone went through unless they would rather die.

So like I said before, I was Kate, Julie and Sadie's prisoner back in the middle 1800s. I knew what they wanted to know; but back then, I couldn't lift a dime without hurting myself; they were strong in comparison. If I were to go back in time though, as I am today, I would have snapped each of them like a *twig without thinking twice. The things those girls did to me are just unforgivable. And today's generation of Kate, Julie and Sadie are exact replicas of their ancestors. But I would say today's generation of the 666 girls are a lot less harsh.*

After I became a vampire, Sage made it clear that I was not to disobey him. He told me what I was and what that meant. Honestly, I don't know why I didn't question it because how would he know what it means to be a vampire? He's human! Even with all of his power and black magic, he's still only human. Technically I am above him on the food chain. What would happen if I ate him? Hmmm…

First I would have to get into hell and then I would have to convince Sage that I was there because of the job he sent me out to do was going in the right direction. I was leading the girls there and then I would have to go for the kill. Would that work? And if it did, would I be able to get out of hell before becoming the only option for the new Devil. It is believed that once The Devil that we have now is dead -truly dead- there has to be another Devil. I don't know if I believe this rumor but I also don't know where it came from so I'm unsure as to if it was part of the stupid curse those girls' ancestors put on Sage to punish him.

There is something that I know and the girls do not. It is that there is one very difficult way into hell that you can also exit through. All the other openings are entrances only. And you have to go in the invisible entrance in order to exit through it; otherwise it's not activated. Once it's activated, it's obvious to all inside and out of Hell. Meaning The Devil would know we're coming. Only way around that is a spell. I know that there is only one possible spell and that would be the specific one that the Sanders sisters used way back when they put The Devil in Hell and threw away the key. It would only give us twenty-four hours to get in, kill Sage, and get out.

There are three ways to get into Hell. Well, technically there are thousands but there are three types of ways. Type one: you earn it by doing something horrible on the surface while you are alive and you don't ask for forgiveness before you die. Then after you die you go to Hell for all eternity instead of Heaven. The good thing about this is that if you get into Hell because of doing something horrible on the surface of the Earth while alive, you know that you deserve going to Hell. Also another benefit is that you can easily get out of going to Hell this way by asking for forgiveness. The bad part though is that even if you ask for forgiveness, you aren't automatically granted it.

Meaning you can ask for forgiveness but you could still go to Hell, still knowing that you somehow deserved it. Type two: you ask to enter, knowing the fact that you will never be able to back out of it. You walk into Hell with permission from The Devil, then you stay in Hell working for him. This way of getting into Hell is by personal choice and you know that you chose it so it's your fault if you regret it. One way to get out of Hell from entering it this way is to become a demon spy like me. I'm working for Sage, gaining the trust of his next most important victims. But am I in Hell? Nope. Type three: You use the invisible entrance. Only a few demons know about this entrance to Hell. The Devil will notice that you are there, eventually, but if you do it right you have to be out of there before twenty four hours has gone by. This is a huge challenge since the time is different in Hell. The good side to this is that you can go in and get out of Hell unnoticed if you're smart about it. The bad side is that you can easily be seen and be trapped in Hell if you mess up the invisible spell.

"Let's go then."

"Hold on Kate, you can't just start fighting. You have to know what you are up against." I explained.

"You said you know how to get into Hell

without it being a permanent vacation, so let's go kill ourselves a Devil."

"I hate to say it, but Tyson is right." Julie started, "Even with my spell, if I find it, I can't promise a way out. You have to go in prepared." *Julie just agreed with me?* Tyson thought.

"I know of a way but it's more complicated then just going in and being invisible to The Devil. We would only have twenty four hours to get in, kill Sage and get out."

"So? What's the big deal? Twenty four hours is way more than we need. I'm talking like twenty minutes maximum."

"You aren't listening!" I yelled. After calming down a little, I continued, "Twenty four hours on the surface of the Earth is a long time, sure, but in Hell it's different. Time is different. Back when Hell hadn't existed yet, Sage used dark magic to play with time. Then when he created the separate Dimension of Hell, he used the time morphing magic to make it seem a lot slower than it really is inside the new world. One hour up here, is almost the equivalent to one day. I'm not exactly sure as to the conversion, though."

"So we would only have one hour to kill Sage

and get out?" Sadie asked me, with a worried expression.

"What are you so worried about? This will be easy!" Kate cheered as she started for the door again, "Twenty minutes maximum. That's all we need."

So...I sort of feel bad because I'm hiding a lot from Kate. And her sisters, but I mostly care about what I'm hiding from Kate. My past, for one, has never been explained because they could, and would, figure out I work for Sage. A couple weeks after meeting the 666 girls, I still haven't mentioned a major person...well vampire, now...in my life and in my undead life.

— — —

Kate

I don't know what it is about my sisters' thoughts on Tyson but I really think they might be right. He seems to be hiding something and I need to know what. I feel like half of him is hidden behind that wall of secrets. How am I supposed to get to know him if he won't tell me anything about him? Like his past? And what is up with Julie? She's been acting very oddly lately...

— — —

Julie

Why is Kate not listening to me? Another question is why am I asking that stupid question? She never listens to me. Why should it surprise me that she's not now? The answer to that is that it doesn't surprise me. What surprises me is that she is in love with a vampire. Not only that but a vampires that is hiding something. I guess I can understand the hiding something thing though, since I myself am hiding a huge fact as well. There's this guy…vampire…that knows Tyson from their childhood of human life and some of baby years as vampires. He's told me a lot about Tyson and most of it is bad stuff to keep to myself. It's killing me not to inform my sisters but I would have to explain how I got the information if I told them. Tyrone is this vampire's name and he considers Tyson a brother even though they aren't related. Though, they probably could be because they look a lot alike too. Anyway, Tyrone has given me some interesting information about Tyson. Somehow I already knew that he and Sage had something to do with each other more so than Tyson was leading on; but I didn't want to crush Kate. Now I'm regretting that because I don't want Tyson to crush her either.

Better someone she knows she loves crush her rather than an undead vampire that she has fallen for way too quickly. Some of the things that Tyrone has told me are things like Tyson working for Sage and Tyson knowing our ancestors. A little better than I would have thought possible. According to Tyrone, Tyson got to the point of dating *Julie of the first generation Sanders' girls. Then he was turned into a vampire and Julie tried to kill him, and in the process, he killed her. Tyrone says that he was ripped up about having to kill her because he loved her. Tyson loved the first generation version of* me! *That's just insane if you ask me. But anyway, Tyrone has given me the permission to tell everyone that I've been in contact with him, but I just don't know how. I know for a fact that Kate would never let me hear the end of secretly meeting with a vampire. And I agree that it's an odd move for me to do but I still don't think it's as bad as falling in love with a vampire.*

—— —— ——

Sadie

I don't know what to do. Tyson is helping us but we don't know if we can trust him, Julie has been acting really odd for the last couple of weeks like she's hiding something, and I feel like I'm so out of the loop. Why can't my sisters inform me on what is going on. Kate has the advantage of being a little closer to Tyson than me and Julie, and Julie has the advantage of being able to get what ever information needed by just seeing it in her head. What do I have?

Chapter 9

"You almost ready with that spell, Julie?" Tyson asked the witch.

"No, actually. I'm not almost ready. I need a dozen supplies and ingredients that I've never even heard of. I don't know where to get half of this stuff and no one here is helping me!" Julie was over stressed and over tired from several nights of sleeplessness. This was all caused by her doing all of the research and all of the 'lab work' while the others fought some strange demons that were lurking about their territory.

"In order for the spell to work, you have to be

powerful enough to do it by yourself. Your ancestor locked Hell all by herself, and she wasn't even close to having your amount of power. You can do this." The spell that Julie was preparing to cast was the invisible spell. It was more of a charm, which made it a lot more difficult to control.

"I may have a lot of power, Tyson, but that doesn't mean I know how to use it...or how to control it." Julie stated. This was the truth. There was more to being a witch than just having power. You had to know how to use that power and control that power for it to mean anything. Sage didn't know that when he performed the black magic that got him trapped in Hell in the first place. Once he started to build on his idea of another dimension, he couldn't control the power and that is what ended up making the new dimension a place of torment in the end. Black Magic Gone Bad. And when you have to admit that *black magic* has gone hay-wire, you know it's a bad situation.

"Point taken, but we need to get this done."

"What's the big hurry, Tyson?" Julie asked with raised eyebrows. She was growing more aggravated and suspicious of rushed Tyson's behavior.

"Just...we don't want to wait until he gets more powerful. Right?" Tyson hesitated.

"Here's a question for you. How does he get stronger? And how do you know that he gets stronger still after all these years. He's a human being. Shouldn't he be like super super old and weak?"

"Sadie, sometimes you are just really not observant." Tyson started, "He's human with Power-Steroids." Tyson chuckled at his own joke, "He's alive and as young as he was when he was first locked in Hell. But now he has six hundred and fifty some souls collected; he needs less then twenty more. The more souls he collects, the stronger he gets. It was part of the curse that your ancestors put on him. They clearly didn't think it through very well."

"How can you know so much about the curse?"

"Stop asking so many questions. Do you have the spell ready, yet?" Tyson was starting to get impatient. The girls didn't really know why, but Tyson was just irritable. 'On edge' was how Kate described it to her sisters. He was mostly acting that way around her and Julie.

— — —

"So where's this entrance you claim to know about, Tyson? Julie is starting the spell like right now, meaning we need to get in there before she is done chanting, right?"

"Why are you in such a rush to go to Hell, Kate? Excited to meet The Devil?" *What is with Tyson? Earlier he was in a huge rush to get out of the house. He was even kind of acting like there was some person or thing that he didn't want to catch up with us. He was rushing Julie into starting the spell and he didn't seem to care that that could possibly mess her up.*

"Oh yeah. Because meeting The Devil and making a deal with him is my secret life long dream, Tyson." Kate answered sarcastically.

"It's not a secret anymore, Kate. Everyone knows you have the hots for Sage. The big and bad."

"That's not true. I have the hots for…" Kate stopped herself but it was too late. Tyson already caught her choice of words and planned on using it against her.

"You have the hots for who, Katie-cat?" Kate despised her new nickname but because she secretly had the hots for Tyson, she also thought it was a cute nickname.

"No one." Kate got really defensive.

"Kate. You should know that I've been alive for a long time and I know how to tell if you are lying. And therefore I know you are lying. Not to mention, if I wanted, I could just read your thoughts to figure it out." His smile widened at Kate's high eyebrows. He could see that she was frightened by the thought of *that* power being in Tyson's hands.

"I don't know what you're talking about, Tyson. You are just making stuff up because you like the thought of me liking someone. The truth is, I don't have time to like someone. So even if I did, I wouldn't say or do anything about it because I have no time." Kate was trying to convince herself of this along with convincing Tyson.

"Keep trying to convince yourself of that, Katie-cat. I know who you have the hots for and I know you are *dying* to show it. Why else did you stay in my basement after I let you go from being my captive?"

"That's besides the point. Where's the entrance?" that's when Sadie tapped Kate on the shoulder and pointed towards a completely dead patch of land.

"Kate. Don't you think that is, at least, a little odd? Everything is alive and then a small, what looks like it could be a five yard diameter, circle of dead land. Dead plants, dead trees. I think that's very…not right." Kate could tell that Sadie, too, knew who she liked and wanted to talk about something else. *Perfect timing noticing the odd dead patch.* Kate thought.

"I've seen this before." Tyson started, "It's a sign of The Devil but it's a trap."

"What do you mean, a trap? Sage knows we're coming?" Kate asked suspiciously, "How could he *possibly* know that we were coming?"

"No! That's not what I mean at all. I mean I have seen this before as a sign that The Devil can come out of Hell for a brief amount of time. It's like a teleporting machine." Tyson started explaining that as Sage comes closer to his needed six hundred and sixty six souls, he grows stronger. And as he gets stronger, Sage can make this sort of teleportation spot that gives him the ability to hop out of Hell for a short amount of time. But in that amount of time, Sage can do anything he wants, as long as he doesn't exit the circle shaped teleportation hot spot. The stronger Sage got, the bigger he could make these hot spots but he seemed to like to keep them at the five yard diameter. This was because if he kept them smaller, he could have several of them spread across the world. The only real way of knowing that it was a Devil hot spot is to look at it carefully. The facts that would prove that is was one of these rare hot spots made by Sage were things such as is it a perfect circle? Is it five to ten yards in diameter? Is every single thing in the circle dead? Are their graves in the circle?

Kate found it very interesting that Tyson knew

that the "Devil Hot Spots" only got up to ten yards in diameter. The only history of these hot spot circles that Tyson knew anything about was long gone in his memories. What he could remember, though, wasn't something that he was just going to share out of the blue just because they came across one little circle. Sage started making these hot spots at a diameter of three yards when he was just past two hundred and twenty two souls into his collection. One third of the way of getting out of his curse gave him the ability to control minds, read minds and create spots on the Earths' surface where he could pop up for a couple minutes. Back then, it was only for a couple minutes. Now, Tyson supposed, Sage could come onto the surface for hours at a time. The true meaning of The Devil hot spots was that he was getting closer. Tyson always knew this day would come.

"You would think since Sage *made* Hell, he wouldn't want to escape it so badly."

"Hell is a horrible place, Sadie. Sage may have been the creator of Hell but he was trapped in there by others. By your ancestors to be exact, and it's not a place to just barge into. If we don't go through the correct entrance, we will be stuck there and you two will be eternally tortured."

"What about you?" Sadie wanted to know. She was curious as to why he specifically pulled himself out of the calculation for that scenario.

"I'm a vampire."

"Your point?" Kate asked.

"I was made to be an evil demon *from* Hell. I was made *from* torture. The worst case would be that they would force me to inflict the torture on you girls. The demons of Hell think of me as one of the torturers. I was made to torture and I was made from torture. But that doesn't matter."

"Why doesn't that matter, Tyson? My sisters and I getting tortured by an evil demon such as yourself doesn't matter? Is it because we aren't demons? And therefore *we* don't matter? What are you trying to say?" Sadie got very aggressive with her accusations.

"Sadie! Calm down! He's not saying that. He's saying at this moment, we are not being held in Hell as captives. We should be careful as to what we say though because if that is in fact a teleporting area for Sage to be able to just pop up out of no where, even for the briefest amount of time, we could be in huge trouble. Tyson, where *is* the entrance?"

Tyson lead the two girls to a hole in the hill. It didn't look like a cave, just a hole or even more like a piece of the hill was scraped away. Kate watched Tyson as he explained that this is where he believed the invisible entrance was. She saw the way he smiled as he saw the expression that her sister had given him when they finally got to stop walking. They had been walking for hours to find the entrance. Even after finding the teleporting area, they had walked at least fifteen miles.

Sadie had wondered on the way if they could just rest for a little bit but Tyson insisted that Sage would try to come out of Hell after dark.

"How do you know that Sage comes out onto the Earth at night and not during the day?" *How the hell does Tyson know all of this? How does he know that The Devil's name is Sage? How does he know that there could be a different Devil out there? How does he know what this circle of complete dead means? Or even what it is? How does he know that Sage will most likely come out at night? How does he know so much about my family's history? How does he know more than me or my sisters about our family? How does he know what I'm about to say when I'm just about to say it? How does Tyson know what he knows? And why won't he just come out with everything that he knows right now! I want to know about his past! I want to know him better!*

— — —

When Sage was a little boy around the age of six, his parents died in a car crash that he just happened to survive. No one knows how Sage survived but ever since then, he has been obsessed with magic because he believed one hundred and thirty percent that magic had caused him to survive the drowning of their car. He remembers seeing his parents spirits rise out of their bodies, wave good bye to him and his sister and then go into a very bright light off in the distance. His little sister died a couple years later due to a sickness that hadn't been named until the recent years. It was an early form of cancer.

As Sage got older, he found no reason to socialize or be a part of the growing world. So instead, Sage just hid in his home playing around with white magic, black magic, easy magic and advanced magic of all sorts. By doing this, Sage made himself more prone to being overthrown by his expanding power. Eventually Sage grew tired of the same old same old magic. He started to try newer things that his books didn't cover or explain. Soon after that, Sage began to experiment with things like space and time. By doing this, Sage's power started to control him, making him unable to stop from continuing to examine what he was capable of. Sage became better at time spells and became more familiar with the space spells. He got to be so good with these that he decided to try and make a whole other world within the atmosphere of Earth.

This is when Hell began to exist. At first it was just supposed to be a dimension to escape to when he couldn't deal with the people around him. But everyone makes enemies, and once Sage started to, he decided to transform his new creation to a prison, basically, for the people he didn't get along with.

That's when the first generation Julie Sanders performed her 666 curse, trapping Sage in his own establishment. Which brings the history to today's version of a very crazy, very cranky, very powerful human that has been trapped for a little under two hundred and ten years and is very close to getting out.

— — —

When Tyson was a young, human boy, he lived with a family that consisted of him and four others. He lived with his mom, Ellen, his dad, Henry, and his two sisters, Madison and Justine. They were all murdered only a couple of days after Tyson's birthday. He hid during the killing but then was found and captured by the killers. From then on, he was trained and taught to believe that vampires ruled the world, and that vampires were the future of the human race. He lived in a home that Sage controlled after becoming obsessed with his power but before he was trapped by it.

The 'home' was Sage's way of collecting a bunch of young people so he could eventually take each of their souls. Either by killing them or by turning them. Sage had a method of doing this. He collected the boys and girls at a very young age, even as young as five years old. By doing that, he could manipulate their minds into thinking that becoming a demon, such as a vampire, Spirit or any other type, is just a part of life. This would make Sage feel less guilty about killing them or turning them into a creature of Evil because they each got a choice.

— — —

"I don't understand how you know all of this, Tyson. All of this information is just…in the least it just seems impossible for you to know all of this just because of the fact that you are a vampire. Not every vampire knows about us and about Sage, do they?"

"Well no," Tyson started, "but I can't really explain it right now."

"Why not, Tyson? Why can't you just come out and tell us everything you know about Sage and about us and about vampires in general?"

"Okay, Kate. I do need to tell you something. But you have to promise me you aren't going to get mad, okay?"

Chapter 10

What is it that I like about him? Tyson is sweet, nice, honest, and gentle. Even when he's trying to be intimidating or manly, he's gentle about it. He's about where he comes from, what he is. I mean even when I first met him, and he thought I was planning on killing him for information, he was sweet about the whole keeping me against my will thing. I don't know why I love Tyson but I know this feeling isn't going away. Not for a while if ever.

Way back in 1890, when Tyson was a sixteen year old boy, he knew the Sanders girls. Sure, he was living in a home that was controlled by vampires and he was being raised by said vampires, but at the time, the Sanders girls weren't yet well known as demon hunters. Instead, they were known as popular school girls; though they did live the secret life of demon hunting on the side. So at age sixteen, Tyson became close friends with the triplets. It even got to the point of him and Julie dating. That stopped as soon as Sage made his deal with Tyson. The first generation Julie took demon hunting really seriously. So serious that she didn't even consider giving vampire Tyson the same chance that she gave human Tyson. As the generations went on, Tyson tried again with Sadie and again with Julie. By generation number eight, Tyson had been together with all three girls.

But this generation, number thirteen, was the only time that Tyson was even remotely honest with the triplet that he was trying to date. He may have started their relationship out with a huge line of lies, but this was also the only time out of all those tries, that Tyson actually knew for sure that he was in love. And this was the only time that he knew exactly how she felt about him.

"Tyson, I don't know that we should talk about this right now." Kate told the vampire that was holding her closer to him then he ever had before. He had just whispered in her ear how he knew Sage. Right then, the truth came out. At least for Kate it did. Sadie still didn't know that Tyson was *made* into the demon he is because of Sage by Sage for Sage. Tyson didn't tell Kate that he was working for Sage but he did mention that Sage technically wasn't the only Devil in existence.

Kate didn't want to get into it because she was anxious to get into Hell and defeat the bastard named Sage. But Tyson had believed that this was the perfect time. Little did the girls know, Tyson was trying to save them from Sage knowing when they were coming in on the attack. He would never expect them during the night time. Tyson wanted to make sure the girls were ready. One mistake could end up resulting in a disaster, and he knew that was going to be the case if the girls didn't listen to him.

"Kate, I think this is the perfect time to get into this. Sage won't expect us at night, but we need to make sure you and Sadie are ready. Sage is the real deal but there is also another Devil out there waiting for the battle. For all we know, Sage is his son and they have joined forces. We need to prepare more. And Julie needs to gain more power."

"So, does that mean that we walked all the way here for nothing?" Sadie complained after eaves dropping on Kate and Tyson. She had been falling behind due to breathlessness and lack of on going strength.

That's when Julie appeared out of no where. But she wasn't alone.

"Tyrone, my man!" Tyson walked up to the vampire that was standing right next to Julie, "How've you been?"

"I've been better." *Who's Tyrone? Well, who ever he is, he doesn't seem to be as excited to see Tyson.* Kate thought to herself.

"Who is this, Tyson?" Kate asked as she and Sadie walked closer to the group.

— — —

"I can answer that." Julie said, "This is Tyrone Dean. He and Tyson grew up together. They are like brothers. I know why Tyson knows where the entrance to Hell is. And I know why he knows the time difference. It's almost unknown throughout the history of demons. Even those among the group that were all changed by Sage, himself. But Tyson knows because Tyson was made by Sage and trained by Sage as were a few others including Tyrone. Sage made Tyson the demon he is today and he could, for all we know, be working for him."

"No way! Tyson wouldn't do that!" Kate shouted but she immediately looked over at Tyson for a response from him.

"Think of it this way," Tyrone said to Kate, "How well do you know Tyson? You know he's a vampire, you know he's not one hundred percent Evil, you know he's a decent guy. That's all personality aspects of him. Do you really know anything about his *childhood*? Or how he became a *vampire*?"

Tyrone Dean was wearing a long brown trench coat on top of tan button up shirt and he looked like he was on his way to a job interview. Tyrone's pants were dark brown almost to the point of black and Kate kept looking him up and down to make sure he was actually there. For some reason Kate felt like this was just a trick being played on them by The Devil and she didn't really understand why no one else was wondering that too. Or maybe they were and just not showing it.

Unlike Tyson, Tyrone was forced to watch his parents get murdered by the creature that later raised him. This, as expected, scarred Tyrone for a long time. He may have been raised by these vampires but he hated them with a very strong passion. Tyrone attempted an escape practically everyday. As he got older, the punishments for trying to escape became more severe. This caused Tyrone to realize he may as well just except that he was stuck.

That's when he met Tyson. They were the same age, in the same position and each had no friends. At the time they were both eight year old human boys. They clicked instantly and became very good friends. From then on, they did everything together including getting punished. Then when they got to age sixteen, Tyson started dating Julie Sanders and wasn't as aware of what she was as Tyrone was. Tyrone was very aware that these were the girls that tried to make the world a better place by killing off vampires. But when Tyrone tried to tell Tyson this, he disregarded the facts. Even after Tyson was turned into a vampire, the only thing that convinced him that Julie was a demon hunter was her trying to kill him after she found out he was in fact a demon.

Kate knew deep down that Tyrone was really there but she had a feeling that he wasn't who he claimed to be.

"Now Tyrone, we don't need to be giving out personal information. I've tried really very hard to forget my past and I would love to keep it that way." Tyson commented as Kate looked from him to Tyrone and back. *I wish Kate would trust me; not that I have given her a reason to.* Tyson thought.

"Why have you tried forgetting? Was it really that bad being my brother?" Tyrone joked. He was joking but he was also very serious.

"You know why I've tried to forget, Tyrone. And it has nothing to do with you. So don't do that thing where you try to get me to confess all of my sins of the past. I have made mistakes and I sometimes wish I could go back and change them. But you and I know I would just go back in time to make the same mistakes all over again," Tyson exclaimed.

"Oh I think I know that better than you do, brother. But I really think you should let these girls know who you really are. It's only fair." Tyrone told Tyson. That's when Tyrone noticed Tyson's reaction to Kate staring at him as though waiting for an explanation, "Oh. I understand, brother, why you haven't come out with the whole truth. But does she know?" *I think Tyson needs to just get it over with and tell Kate and her sisters the truth. Not even her sisters. Kate is the one that needs to hear it because she needs to know who she is falling in love with.* Tyrone reflected.

"Tyrone, I miss you man, but why are you here?" Tyson changed the subject. This made Kate sigh and Tyrone chuckle a little. Julie smiled at Tyrone only because she knew Tyson's little secret and has known it almost since they first allowed him to come along and help them. And Tyrone knew that she knew. But did Tyson?

"I was getting a little…thirsty …and saw this helpless little girl walking on the side walk alone and about to go through an alley way. She was only going to be a snack but when I went for the bite, she came back at me with a full blast of black magic! She's strong. We got to talking and she teleported us here." Julie smiled a little wider this time before speaking.

"When he says 'we got to talking', he really means he threatened me to tell him where Tyson was and I refused a couple times before teleporting us here. And because I know my sisters so well, I will answer your question before you ask it. Yes I teleported both him and I at the same time with no help from any demons, demonettes, gods or goddesses. Tyrone is the reason I know I can do that now."

Tyrone had contacted Julie a few months back through a mysterious phone call. Never did they ever meet in person until that evening in the alley way. Tyrone was not aware that it was Julie Sanders, the 666 witch that he was about to snack from.

Kate noted that Julie's voice was a little weaker than normal and that's when she saw the fang marks on her neck.

"You let him bite you?" Kate demanded. *So now she's being judgmental when it comes to being a vampires' snack? What are those marks on her wrists, hmm? And her neck is covered in pairs of vampire fangs! How dare she!* Tyrone screamed in his head. He wanted to object to Kate's comment aloud but that would be rude and he was to stay calm during this whole meeting.

"Don't even try to tell me you haven't let *that* thing bite you! I've seen it. And you have multiple scars as proof." Julie jumped at Kate's accusation.

"That's different." Kate argued.

"How is that different, Kate!"

"It's different because I didn't have a choice. I was trying to use Tyson at the time. I was trying to get information out of him so I made a trade. I did it for the team. You did it for pleasure."

"How in Hell would you know why I let Tyrone bite me? You weren't there and you can't read minds."

"Girls. Is this really that important? We should be focusing on something else." Tyrone commented mostly to Kate because Julie already knew this. They both already knew this but Kate was the one that started the irrational behavior about being bitten by a vampire ally.

What Kate, Sadie and Tyson all didn't know was that Julie and Tyrone had been in contact for almost the last five months. Tyrone had contacted her as soon as he heard Tyson was planning to enter into their lives. This wasn't really important for everyone to know but what Julie wanted to share was that Tyrone's blood had given her some of these more advanced skills in the black arts. She had just recently agreed to drinking from him to enhance her strength but then when his blood started to give her more power in the magic, she wanted more of it to see what she could do; so she could understand how much she could handle. This was all in the last day when they first met in person in that alleyway.

Tyrone Dean wasn't telling the whole truth either. The history of Tyrone was a secret even to Tyson. Tyrone wasn't working for Sage but he had his own dark secrets he didn't plan on exposing.

— — —

Why do I love you so? What is it about you that makes my heart stop every time your eyes meet mine? What feature on your beautiful face makes me smile whenever I see you? What part of your absolute perfect body makes me want you so? Why do I need you in my life? Why do you have to be so damn bad for me? For my instincts? Why do you have to be so damn wrong? All the time; that's how much I think of you. That's how much I imagine being with you. What's wrong with me? I can't seem to say it out loud. Not even when I'm alone. Am I embarrassed? Am I unsure? I can't be unsure because I'm positive of my feelings for you. And I shouldn't be embarrassed because you are him. I can feel it. You are the guy I'm supposed to be with. The guy I'm meant to be with. I've known you for how long, Tyson? I've known you for only weeks, not completely sure how many. This is ridiculous. How, in that short amount of time, can I know you are the one?

"Tyson, you and I need to talk." Kate said. This statement got Julie to teleport the rest of them out of there. Where they went, Kate and Tyson didn't know. Tyrone had fed on Julie, this was true, but it didn't stop there. Tyrone informed the 666 witch that vampire blood could hype her powers as a witch and as a human being. It makes the average human's senses become very strong, not only that but it would potentially make Julie gain several more and different powers that she had been working towards. Because of this, when Julie took even one swallow worth of Tyrone's two hundred year old vampire blood, she was able to teleport with no help needed from the demonettes or goddesses. The more she drank, the more she could do. Including the growing power of teleportation. She only had to take three swallows full of his blood to be able to teleport multiple people without any physical contact with any of them. Just a snap of the fingers and off they went.

For a brief second, Kate wondered if Tyrone had been the reason for the sudden power that Julie had discovered but then she forced herself to focus on the topic at hand; her feelings for Tyson. *How do I start?* She asked herself. Tyson stared at Kate for a brief minute then he opened his mouth to talk. He paused before saying anything but he was only trying to find the right words. Tyson knew exactly what this was about.

"Kate, I don't think you should say what you are about to say." Tyson commented.

"How do you know what I'm going to say? You know, this would be a lot easier if you could read minds."

"Kate…" another pause, "I have something I need to tell you." Tyson started.

Chapter 11

"Okay, now it's my turn for confessions. I don't really know how obvious I've been about it but you may have noticed I sort of like you."

"I'm a likable vampire. It's not your fault." Tyson joked. *Why does he always have to joke around? It's so annoying. Cute, but annoying. Is he taking me seriously? Should I tell him? Is it the right thing to do?*

"Clearly I haven't been very obvious if you don't know what I'm getting at." Kate commented under her breath. She crossed her arms in frustration. *This would be a perfect time for Tyson to have mind-*

reading powers. She thought.

"No, Kate, I know where you are going with this. But can you just say it out loud and stop acting afraid?" Tyson inquired.

"Afraid? Of what? I'm not afraid." Tyson just started to walk away, expecting Kate to jump up and just say what she had to say as soon as he did, "Wait! Tyson!" Tyson turned around and smiled. *It worked.* Tyson chuckled to himself, "Okay Tyson, I … I have feelings for you. I don't know why and I can't seem to justify them but I think I have had them since like a week into you holding me captive." *Why is confessing how I feel so hard?*

"And it's been obvious since then." Tyson commented. He chuckled again. *There he goes joking around again.*

"Do you want to talk about it? I mean, you haven't really said anything in return to make me feel like I did the right thing by telling you." Kate remarked.

"You did the right thing by telling me. I already knew, but it's nice to hear it." Tyson laughed slightly, "Kate, do you know why I agreed to going along with your little group of so-called demon hunters?" Kate shook her head but then answered.

"I thought it was because you wanted to help

us…"

"Well, let's just put it this way. It started out as a joke to me. I kept you captive for three days and you stayed an extra week, purely because you wanted to. Even back then I could tell that you liked me. Don't get me wrong, I like having this attention but I had been wondering why for a while now. I was going to come out and just ask you but that's when I saw how you treat the demons you don't like, so I decided to just go along with it. By that time, we had gotten to know each other a little bit. I started to like you, your personality and your family. Now I'm still by your side because I don't like Sage. I want to tell you everything I know about him but I can't and I have reasons for that that I also can't tell you."

"Why not?" Kate questioned. Kate's hands were now on her hips as her expression became filled with worry and anger.

"Because Sage and I have more to do with each other than you know. I'm not supposed to say anything. Kate… you have to believe me when I say I care about you. I do. And it's wrong."

"Why is it wrong? Why does it have to be wrong?"

"I'm a vampire that has a reputation to uphold and I can't … let's go to my place to talk about this. There are people around listening to us."

"*What* people, Tyson!" they were still standing on the top of the hill by the entrance to Hell and Tyson was claiming that he could hear people around them. These people were actually there and they were people that Tyson didn't want to hear this particular conversation. These eavesdropping people worked for Sage as well and were just 'checking in' on Sage's most loyal vampire- Tyson.

"You can't hear them because you're human. Come on, my place is just over the hill." Tyson insisted. *He lives by the entrance to Hell? I might be just reading into this but that seems a little odd.*

The two of them made their way to Tyson's apartment and Kate just stared at the inside and at how clean it was in comparison to her house.

"Tyson can we just talk? I don't want this to go on and on, so I'm just going to say it. I have feelings for you that have been growing for a long time. I don't know why and I can't justify them...but I shouldn't have to. I know that you like me at least as a person too and I know that we can do something about it."

"Why do you have to be able to justify them?" Tyson asked, "What do you suggest we do, Kate? We can't start dating. I have a reputation to uphold. Like I said before. And my life is just...too complicated for you."

"For me? What do you mean by that, Tyson?

Too complicated for me to *handle*?"

"Yes but that's not what I was trying to say, but that too. You live a really complicated life with all of your demon hunting and you can't just expect me to agree to adding to that complication. I'm a demon, am I not?"

"You are but you aren't like other demons." Kate claimed. *I want Tyson to kiss me already!*

"How am I any different than Tyrone, or Sage for that matter? I'm a vampire, and I kill humans in order to survive. I have to feed off of you because I need human blood to stay strong. How is that different from *other* demons? How am I different than the demons you kill for a living?" Tyson disputed.

"It's different because I've never agreed to having a demon help us out like this before. I've never basically forced my sisters to trust a guy that held me captive. I've never gone alone on a job and come out with this type of relationship with a demon. Tyson just tell me one thing. Do you have feelings for me too, or is this just all in my head?" there was a long pause and Kate just got more annoyed. She went to the other room and sat down on the edge of the bed. The sheets were red and there was a black comforter on top of them pulled back neatly.

Tyson walked into the bedroom, "Do you feel more comfortable in here?" he grinned widely.

"Stop that. Don't joke about it like it means nothing to you."

"Why do you think I'm joking?" Tyson asked, "Listen, Kate, I know I shouldn't get involved with a demon hunter because I've been down this road before. With Julie, actually."

"With Julie?"

"You're ancestor named Julie Sanders. We tried dating when I wasn't a demon and then during our relationship was when I was turned. She tried to kill me. I don't think I should take that chance again. But that doesn't mean I don't want to." Tyson slowly made his way over to Kate on the bed and he sat down next to her. She scooted a little away but Tyson only scooted towards her. He put his arm around her waist making her unable to move away anymore.

"So what are you saying?"

"I have feelings for you too. I just don't think we should go through with making anything out of it."

"Why not?" Kate whined a little, jokingly. She could tell that Tyson wasn't lying about this, "I have fallen for you, you have at least some feelings for me. I don't see why we can't just…" Tyson started to lean in for a kiss.

"Katelyn Elizabeth Sanders. I'm surprised you would be fooled by such a creature. Aren't you supposed to be the thirteenth generation of the leader in the all time feared Sanders 666 group? The future of the girls who trapped me in Hell? And you fall for *that* guy? I'm dumbfounded!" Kate quickly turned her head away from Tyson and towards the corner of the room. There stood Sage. He was standing in a circle of torn up carpet. *I thought it was only outside that those hot spots could be formed?* Kate asked herself.

"Who the hell are you?" Kate paused for a moment and looked more carefully at the man that interrupted her first kiss with Tyson. "Oh my god! You're Sage!" Kate looked from Sage to Tyson and back. That's when Sage spoke again; this time to Tyson.

"Oh, and dear boy. You would think after multiple tries with a Sanders girl you would stay away from that kind of trouble."

"What?" Kate asked Tyson, "*Multiple?*"

"That's not important. Sage, go back to where you came from!"

"Why, dear boy? Do you not appreciate me saving you the trouble of telling your sweetheart the truth?"

"Truth?" Kate asked Tyson, this time with anger

growing in her expression and voice.

"The truth about why he has been so called helping you this whole time, dear Katelyn. He's been working for me as an under cover spy, gaining your trust so in the end he could give you to me and set me free, causing Hell to come onto Earth and for humans to be under the control of all demons and, of course, me." Sage paused and took a step forward. The circle of ripped carpet became bigger as he came closer to the couple on the bed, "You didn't actually think any of the information Tyson gave you was truth, did you? You don't really believe that he cares about you?" Sage's expression showed a challenge to answer that question.

"Kate, don't listen to him. I really do care about you. At first it was about that but I chose to stop working for him a long time ago."

"When? When were you going to tell me that you were working for The Devil?" Kate demanded, "And when were you going to tell me that you changed your mind about it? I thought you were being honest with me, Tyson! How am I supposed to trust you now?"

"Never trust the undead, dear Katelyn. Didn't your mother teach you that?" Sage laughed, "Oh that's right, your mother is dead. And so is your daddy-o. Poor little Katelyn; has no parents to teach her the necessities in life."

"Stop it! I could take you out right here, if I wanted to!"

"You know that's not true. Now, how about we let me finish what I was saying earlier. I was telling you about how your little almost-lover has been working for me since I changed him into a vampire. He's the only one that stayed loyal all these years. What has it been, a couple hundred?" Sage looked at Tyson briefly and then back to Kate, "I sent him after you three girls each time a new generation of you were born. You are the only generation that seemed to actually believe he was capable of good."

"I *am* capable of good. Kate you have to believe me. I love you." Tyson tried.

Kate got up from the bed and stormed out of the room, tears running down her face. She started to pace out in Tyson's living room, and she started to evaluate if Tyson's betrayal mattered to her. She had true feelings for him and she knew better than a lot of people that everyone makes mistakes that they regret.

I don't know what I should do, Kate thought, *can I trust what Sage is saying? Tyson doesn't seem to be denying it. Is that because it's all true? I can believe that he was turned by Sage because that part makes sense; that's why he knows so much. But Gust made it really clear that Tyson was the only man that could possibly know everything about Sage. He also could have been lying, that bastard has a habit of doing that.*

*But I have feelings for Tyson and I should stick with my
instinct. Of course that has been messed up ever since
I met Tyson so what should I do?*

Kate wasn't angry at Tyson for lying to her or
betraying her and her family; and she wasn't sad that
her first love started their almost-relationship off with a
huge line of lies. Kate was scared. Scared that she
might be making a mistake by saying good bye to her
first love, afraid that Sage might be making some of
this up because who knew if she could trust him. Kate
was afraid because neither her nor her sisters figured
out that Tyson was against them the whole time. Or so
she thought.

*They would have told me if they knew,
wouldn't they?* She started to question the loyalty of
her sisters now too. Who could she trust now that she
knew that Tyson had been lying the whole time? How
could she know who was on her side? Now that
Tyson's secret of betrayal was out in the open between
him and Kate, would they be able to continue having
feelings for each other? Was his claim of loving her the
truth? Or was it just to get her to fall for him all over
again? These questions ran through Kate's head as she
paced some more. A couple minutes later she
reentered the bedroom, where Tyson and The Devil
awaited. They hadn't moved.

"So you clearly came here for a reason, Sage.
What is that reason?" Kate asked while standing

stationary in the doorway.

"I have enough power to leave Hell and create Hell on Earth." Sage claimed.

"It's kinda funny that I don't believe that." Kate still stood at the doorway of the room, "But what's even more funny is I don't even think you believe that, because that was the lamest attempt at convincing someone that I have ever seen. Everyone in this room knows you need a Sanders' Soul to be freed. And at least two of the three of us know that you aren't going to get it."

"Tell me this dear Katelyn, does the fact that your first true love has betrayed you already really not bother you that much? Come on, I think *he* deserves the truth too."

"Tyson is..." Kate glanced at Tyson with a tear almost about to roll down her cheek again. But she kept it in her eye because she knew things would some how work out, "Tyson is a good guy, a sweet vampire and a not evil being. People make mistakes all the time. Sometimes those mistakes are hidden from others for a very long time and sometimes those people don't deserve a second chance to prove that they can change." Tyson was staring at Kate the whole time she spoke. She started to walk towards him as she continued but he was motionless, "Tyson is a great person and he has been to that place of mistakes and back. He's already proven to me and my family that he can be trusted with our lives in his hands. I don't think that a one time betrayal will have to come between us if he doesn't want it to." Now Kate and Tyson were holding hands. But then Kate turned her head towards Sage, "So, Sage, to answer your question. Tyson double crossing me was probably just the stepping stone we needed to lift off whatever type of relationship we have going for us."

"I have to say, dear Katelyn, I didn't expect you to be okay with a liar."

"Everyone lies, Sage. So, why are you here?" this time it was Tyson asking the question, only to prove that he was no longer on Sage's side.

I hope I'm doing the right thing by staying with the good. Sage had promised me power; more than I could imagine but I get such a rush when I'm with Kate and her sisters. And now I can catch up with Tyrone. I haven't seen him in over thirty years. Is this the right thing to do? I guess it's kind of too late because I've already decided to stay with Kate. I think I love her. True love isn't supposed to be possible for a vampire like me. At least, that's what I've been told. But she made it real.

"I'm here to collect the soul that you owe me." Sage announced, his voice became deeper as he started to rise from the carpet. Kate and Tyson ran outside of the house and onto the side walk because Tyson believed that this was a safer plan to be out in the open. But Sage followed them, "I may not be strong enough to escape Hell's boundaries yet but I am strong enough to cause Hell to happen out here. And I don't think you want me to do that, dear Katelyn, because your family is first on the list to experience Hell's torture." They were standing on the sidewalk in the middle of a neighborhood. The windows on the nearby houses started breaking, causing the families inside to either scream their lungs out or run outside.

Kate looked at Tyson for help but he didn't understand what she was about to do, "What can I do to make that not happen? What do you want from me?"

"Would you like to make a deal with The Devil?"

Chapter 12

Tyson

A deal with The Devil is known to work like a contract with your soul as the negotiation. But that's not how it really works. I know from personal experience that a deal with The Devil is much more than just handing over your soul so you can have riches or a new car. In the movies you see the stupid human asking for something they could eventually get on their own if they worked at it and trading it for their soul instead. They used a deal with The Devil as an easy way out for life's accomplishment.

In my case, I got turned into a vampire because I was 'chosen' out of the other children that day to either cross over or die; and by 'cross over' I mean be turned into a blood sucking demon that fed on every living human being around me, especially family. I had no choice, and I got nothing in return. But my past is a little messed up to begin with.

The deal that Sage is trying to make with Kate is a little different. She doesn't personally get anything out of it but basically it's her for the world or the world for her. So he's asking her if she's selfish or selfless and he already knows the answer; I do too.

Sage is a very powerful man and he has powers that Julie Sanders couldn't even imagine having. This is only because he's collected the innocent souls of over six hundred men, women and children all for his own purpose of getting out of Hell. With every soul that he collects, Sage gains an ounce more power. At the point of gaining ounce by ounce of power, you then have every power in existence and are just adding to it by adding strength and control to it. But only to a point. Sage has past that point and is now losing control but gaining more power. That started as he got past three hundred souls.

Sage can do a lot with his power. One thing that we are witnessing now, actually, is the power to appear out of Hell for a brief amount of time in specific places on the Earth's surface. Creating holes between the dimensions is a very difficult thing to do and a very dangerous thing to do. Sage has the power to control others as well; specifically others that he's turned into demons, like myself.

I know Sage is tricking Kate; but he's using his power on me to keep me quiet. Otherwise by now I would be screaming at Kate to not take the deal. Some way and some how we would be able to defeat him eventually. But because he's using his power on me, to shut me up, I have to just stand here and say nothing until after she's made her decision.

At the same time as wanting Kate to be selfish, I also want her to be a vampire like me so if we have a real thing starting with these mutual feelings for each other, we could be together for eternity instead of only forever. I know that that is super selfish of me to say but I'm a little unsure about how our relationship will turn out if she's only human. But I also want her to be turned by me so I want her to say no to giving her soul to Sage because I want to be the reason she turns- not the world.

My worry still is that no matter what Kate's decision is, Sage will still take her soul and be set free and that's how he'll put Hell on Earth. Because at the moment, there is *no possibility* that he could do such a thing without the last soul that he needs in his collection. Soul number six hundred and sixty six has to be a Sanders' soul; but more specifically it has to be Kate's' soul.

— — —

Tyson and Kate were standing next to each other on the side walk while Sage was a couple feet away on the grass. The three of them were in the middle of a neighborhood that, as a whole, was freaking out because of the floating man and the two people watching the floating man right in front of their houses. All the windows were broken and Sage had even gone as far as starting two houses on fire. If anything else unusual happened, there would be more questions. Trees and bushes decorated the outside of each off-white house and the houses looked almost identical to each other. Kate kept looking at Tyson for help on her decision, not knowing that he physically could not say anything to her at the moment.

— — —

Sage is a human being. He was a human with

way advanced magic powers that go way above being a witch. He is, in a way, respectable for the amount of power he has. If he didn't use his powers for evil starting in the 1890s, Sage would have had a lot of potential. Potential to be the most powerful leader of the good in the world. But because of his power addiction, Sage is trapped. He's not only trapped in his own Hell dimension courtesy of the first generation Sanders girls, but he's also trapped in the power addiction that took him over a long time ago. That's why the girls have to defeat him. If Sage were to ever get free from Hell, he wouldn't be able to stop himself from trying to take over the world.

— — —

"I'll give you a choice between two options, dear Katelyn. Option one: you give me your soul and you agree to become a vampire like Tyson. In return, I will not show the world my wrath and I will just become a member of society. I won't put Hell on Earth and I won't cause any harm towards you or your family." Sage paused to let Kate ponder this option. She didn't like it.

Yeah, like that's gonna happen. Kate thought, *I'd rather die than set Sage free. Tyson would probably say do it because he probably wants me turned but if he loves me he'll wait and turn me himself if I choose that path in the future. And what would Julie and Sadie say to this deal? I don't want to be a vampire. As many perks as there may be to being a vampire, I'd rather not kill my sisters out of the first weeks' blood lust. Come on, Sage, what's option two?*

"Option two is you refuse to give me your soul so therefore I show the world my wrath and you suffer along with the world under my control. In this case I will be using you and your sisters and Tyson, here, as my own personal slaves. No doubt in my mind says that you would all end up killing yourselves by the time a week goes by. But with my power I would make you just come back to life so you can suffer some more."

Kate just looked at Tyson as a response to what Sage had explained: the deal with The Devil. The world's fate seemed to lay in Kate's hands alone. Would she let the world be controlled by a man so powerful he made his own Hell Dimension long ago? Or would she give up her soul, become a demon like Tyson, and risk losing herself in the demon only to let the world be free of The Devil? Kate was astounded by the choices she had to choose between. The benefits of both sides of the deal were limited and she knew she didn't have a lot of time to make up her mind.

The deal, as Sage described it was a deal of a life time; literally. Kate had to choose to either let the world suffer under the power of Sage the oh-so-powerful Devil or she had the choice to give him her soul and in return would be 'saving the world from Hell.'

"Tick tock, dear Katelyn. We don't have all day. What's your decision?" Sage pushed.

If I give him my soul, wouldn't that set him free? And if he's set free, can I trust that he's going to keep to his word of not making Hell on Earth? But if I don't give him my soul, could he possibly already have the power to put Hell on earth? These questions were overflowing Kate's thoughts and she didn't understand that she actually had a choice. Kate quickly said her decision out loud right as Tyson thought of a way to make her see that she did have a choice. But it was too late.

Chapter 13

There was a slight pause again before Kate spoke, "Fine. The world needs me, I'll save it over myself. The world deserves a second chance at making life worth while."

"Kate!" Tyson yelled as Sage began to glow with red and black power. Black is the color that represents darkness. When someone as powerful as Sage is floating in mid air and glowing with a black aura around him, it means their intensions are dark. Red is obsession and power. So when Tyson and Kate saw red and black power around Sage, they knew he was

still obsessed with his power. *This isn't a good thing.*
Tyson thought.

Uh oh Kate's eyes widened

Some of the houses around them had open
doors so the families could clearly see the supernatural
event going on in their front yards. Kate's expression
turned from heroic-happy to fear in an instant. She
realized that she'd been tricked. When Kate and Tyson
saw Sage's aura grow with black and red sparks, they
knew Sage planned on destroying the Earth as they
knew it despite the deal Kate had just agreed to.

— — —

Kate Sanders

Why aren't Julie and Sadie here? I could definitely have used their opinion on this situation. Did I make the right decision? Did I act too quickly? Should I have forced conditions on the deal? My sisters should be here and the fact that they aren't is really bothering me. What if something happened to *them*. What is going to happen to me? I just gave up my soul in order to save the world. Did I really just agree to be a vampire? Was that the sane thing to do? Are Julie and Sadie going to be mad at me? What does being a vampire really mean? How long will my first blood lust last? I really wanted my sisters by my side during this. It would be helpful. I don't even care that they probably wouldn't be able to do anything to help. I just want them here, for supportive reasons. Julie should be able to do something by magic. She could help by performing a spell of some sort, right? Wouldn't that work? We could turn back time and un do this thing called turning me into a vampire. I don't want to be a vampire. I don't know why I chose to save the world over my soul. I do, actually, now that I actually think about it. I know why I chose them over me. It's because the world, unfortunately, is more important than I am. The world is full of people, and demons, that deserve a second chance. But do I really deserve to lose my soul in order to give them that second chance? What have I done?

— — —

Sadie Sanders

We wouldn't be able to do anything for her. But I'm worried that Kate is going to be mad. She always has the tendency to get upset over the smallest things so I wouldn't be surprised if she was mad that we weren't there to support her. Because this situation that all of us are in right now…it's not small so she would have good reason to be upset that we're not there for her. But at the same time, I don't think that she should be upset with us because we attempted to save her with that spell. We didn't know that it wasn't going to work. Maybe it did work. Maybe it worked but we, as the spell casters, wouldn't be able to tell by feeling different. Like, maybe, it somehow killed Sage once and for all. Yeah. That's what I think happened.

— — —

Julie Sanders

I couldn't say anything. I couldn't ruin it for my sisters. If they knew from the start about Sage and Tyson, Kate would have never found out who her true love was or who she truly wants to be as a person. Sadie wouldn't have grown stronger and I never would have met Tyrone. I knew all this was going to happen and I wish I could have prevented some of it.

Why does she always have to be the heroine? Why can't she just wait for me to find a spell that can defeat that stupid man that claims to be The Devil. I know for a fact that he's not the real Devil. He's not even the son of The Devil or working for The Devil. Tyson tried to tell her that Sage was the least of our problems but running off and handing over her soul is just not the answer that is going to solve everything- or anything for that matter.

As a witch, I have to keep secrets from my sisters. Like the fact that I can see the future and therefore knew that Sage was going to propose a deal and Kate was going to stupidly take the deal; yeah I knew that was going to happen the second I met Tyson. But if I had said anything about it, I would have either forced Kate to make the other choice and possibly end man kind, or I would just cause Kate to want to make the bad decision even more, but in the process she would question it.

Truth is, Kate is meant to make a quick and stupid decision without the help of Tyson, Sadie or myself. Thirteenth generation Kate is meant to fall for Tyson and is meant to be heart broken by him only to prove that that doesn't matter to her. Everything happens for a reason.

It's hard being the witch in the family. Tyrone and I have had a secret meeting every week since Tyson came into our lives. Tyrone is Tyson's childhood friend and has let me in on some secrets. I trust Tyrone fully with my life and I can slightly understand why Kate is doing what she's doing. I understand a little why Kate believes she has no choice but to give her soul away for the fate of the world? Why couldn't she just wait to see if there was another choice?

Being a witch comes with it's positives and negatives. One thing that is helpful and annoying about witchcraft is that with the help of vampire blood, I can have more powers such as seeing into the future. This is amazing because I never even dreamed of that power. Because of this power, though, I knew all along what the deal with the 'Devil' was going to be and I knew what decision Kate was going to make. I didn't do anything about it because the slightest change in the future can change the whole world. Sounds cliché I know, but it's true.

Tyson has a past of violence and vengeance according to Tyrone. Tyrone told me that Tyson takes all his anger out on the people that are closest to him. He doesn't mean to but it comes with having no soul.

Tyson and Tyrone grew up together. Since they were five year old human beings they've been like brothers. Tyrone is older than Tyson by a week and was always in the older brother position. Both Tyson and Tyrone lived with no parents or biological siblings because they were captured and killed. Tyrone had to watch his family get killed but Tyson hid when it happened to him. They were raised by vampires starting at the age of five and were taught to follow every word. The punishment of not doing so was death.

As they got older though, Tyrone said they started to grow apart and Tyson started showing true hatred towards Tyrone's other friends. Tyrone confronted Tyson about this right before Tyson was called out to be brought to 'The Master'.

The Master was someone that each week was brought a different kid from the group. Some thought of it as an honor to be 'chosen' but those who knew the truth about what went on when you got called out, knew it wasn't good.

That's when Tyson met The Devil. I mean Sage, of course, not the other Devil. And that's when Sage offered Tyson a deal. Die or Cross Over to the Undead part of life. That's what it was to these kids; just another part of life. When you turn seventeen - that's when you got to be part of the drawing to be chosen. Becoming a vampire or another type of demon was just a part of life. You had a choice but it was cross over or die and most chose to live for eternity.

But Tyson's deal was different. Sage saw potential in him. In the end Tyson chose the path of eternal life. But his eternal life was going to be spent serving Sage. As a spy on the Earth's surface. At this time, Tyson was dating my ancestor Julie Sanders generation number two. This was after generation number one obviously so that means Sage had already been trapped in his own creation dimension that he called Hell.

Back to now though, I know that there is something I can do to help my sister out, I just don't know what. I know it's a large risk because I could change the whole future of mankind, but who is to say that isn't a good thing? So there *is* something that I can do to help, but I don't know what it is. I don't know how to find out either. Is it in one of my books? Is it even a spell or charm? Does the help that Kate and Tyson need have anything to do with magic? From all my research on magic, I'm sure I can find a spell or charm or hex that can either trap Sage in Hell again or kill him once and for all. But at the same time, do we *really* want that. I have a feeling that's not the right thing to do…

— — —

"We can't just show up with no plan." Julie explained to her sister.

"We can't just stay here, either." Sadie argued, "Is there something magic based that could help?"

"We've been looking all morning." Tyrone commented.

"Julie, hand me that book. The one of the bottom called *The Advanced*." Julie handed the spell book to her sister in agreement that she and Tyrone could use Sadie's help with the research. So far, said research was a waist of time.

Chapter 14

"Slight change in plans," Sadie announced after realizing that there had to be something wrong with Kate and Tyson because they hadn't come back yet. Only Julie knew what Kate and Tyson were up to at the moment. Not even Tyrone knew that his old friend and the leader of the 666 group were about to face Sage in the most paranormal looking event in history. Julie did know this, though, and she knew there was nothing she could do about it. Not physically anyway. Sadie didn't understand that the two love birds were still gone because they were trying to either save the world or save themselves. She didn't know about the impossible decision her older sister had to make. But

Sadie did know something was up and she knew that Julie wasn't telling her something.

"What are you talking about, Sadie?" This announcement was also because Sadie found a spell that didn't have a name and something inside her told her that it was the spell that could do something.

"There has to be…something's up. They should be back by now." Sadie gave Julie her worried look and Julie sighed. She had hoped that Sadie would just stay out of it but she couldn't help but think that she was going to need Sadie in the end. Julie felt guilty for keeping secrets but at the moment she also knew as a fact that Sadie wouldn't be able to forgive her and then they wouldn't be able to work together; something they really needed to do. Julie had been keeping secrets from her sisters for a while and she knew that her sisters had been hiding things as well. They all had their reasons and they would just have to sit down and talk about it. Later, they would just have to share what it is they'd been hiding and why. Julie knew that if Sadie helped out with spells to help Kate in anyway, even though that was the most logical thing to do, she would somehow suspect or find out some of Julie's more deep kept secrets. This was because they were sometimes written within her self made spells and charms.

"I have something to say." Julie said to her sister,

"I can see them. There is definitely something up but we can't do anything about it at the moment. Kate has to make up her own mind. If we help her, it could change the whole future. She's already made her decision but is hesitating to speak it."

"What are you talking about, Julie? You can't just claim to be able to see them from here and not explain that." *Lately I've been feeling very left out. Tyrone is not trust worthy if you ask me and Julie has been acting…just odd. Honestly, I don't know who to trust anymore. My own sister is keeping secrets from me, and most likely from Kate too. Secrets like powers that let her "see" like that. Why. This just makes me wonder what secrets Kate keeps from us too.* Sadie thought.

"Okay…you want an explanation? I'm a witch. There's your explanation."

"How did you two meet? Why is it that you just happen to know so much about Tyson and how is it that you just happen to know one of his childhood friends?" Sadie was getting suspicious of Julie and that's when Julie changed the subject.

"Sadie, I met Tyrone like literally two weeks after we found Kate in Tyson's bar. He contacted me because he heard that the 666 group had contact with his old friend from his childhood. I know a lot about

Tyson because Tyrone and I have a trusting relationship. I know a lot about Tyson's past and I know about Sage. Sage made Tyson under the agreement that Tyson would work for him for eternity. The only reason Tyson was helping us out is because he wanted to gain our trust and trick us into eventually setting Sage free. But we don't need to focus on that. We need to focus on helping Kate. I have an idea of what spells to try. Tyrone and I will go try them really quick."

"I want to help."

— — —

"So what spell are we going to do next?" Tyrone asked as Julie realized that maybe calling on a god or goddess would be *faster*.

"No spell. Demonette. Specifically, Ellison."

"What's she the demonette of?" Tyrone asked because he had never heard of Ellison. That would be because Julie made her. With all of the powers that Julie has, she was far enough in power to create, manifest and add to the world through black magic and white magic. Julie had made Ellison through curiosity of how much power she had since she's drank from Tyrone. Tyron's blood is over two hundred years old. With vampires, their blood gets more powerful and stronger with years and with abilities. Tyrone has a couple special abilities up his sleeve and the age of his blood gives him the ability to heal himself, others and give powerful witches such as Julie extra powers as well. But sometimes, the witches extra power is only for a temporary amount of time. Julie knows that vampire blood can have that effect of witches as strong and powerful as her, so she figured it was a huge probability that he gave her some of the new powers she'd been experiencing.

"She is a demonette that I created and I think she can do like anything. I don't really know because I've not really tested that theory."

"Do you really think you should test that theory on your *sister*?" Sadie asked, "What if something bad happens?"

"Sadie, don't worry about it. I made her to be pure good." Julie remarked.

That statement made Tyrone's expression turn dark. His eyes grew in disbelief and he snorted, "Nothing is purely good, Julie. You should know that better than most. ...But let's call up this demonette of yours anyway..." Tyrone suggested.

— — —

"Demonette Ellison. Demonette of life, of good, of joy, of the pure, I call on thee. I need thy help. Come forth to me." Julie opened her eyes after finishing the calling, "That didn't go as planned." She commented as over twenty different demonettes, gods, and goddesses came forth.

"We thought we would save you the trouble of calling each of us individually. You don't need us. Any of us. Therefore we will not help you. You are too powerful for the help of gods, goddesses or demonettes and you will forever more be too powerful. We forbid you to call upon us again." They announced as one a moment before disappearing.

"Told you it wasn't going to work." Sadie stuck her tongue out at her sister.

"We'll just have to try to find a spell."

Something inside me is telling me that this spell is going to work. I don't know what it'll do, I don't know why it's nameless and I don't know why I know it's the only spell that will do anything to help my sister. I just do. I can't explain it. What I want to know though is why is it nameless? What does it being nameless mean? Does it even have any significance? Why do I feel this way about it? What's the worst that could happen if we do perform it? Okay, wow, that's a scary thought. But what's gonna happen if it doesn't work? Sadie told herself.

— — —

Kate and Tyson were trying to think of what they could do about Sage floating in front of them and in front of a lot of unknowing humans. Could they make up a story? As Kate thought of something and was just about to say it out loud, she had a sudden stomach cramp worse than any she'd ever experienced before. She screamed. Over half the neighbors had the police on the phones by now and suddenly Tyson noticed a news helicopter overhead. *There's no way we are going to be able to hide this from the world seeing it.* Tyson thought.

Sage was still floating and now surrounded by red and black power and freedom. At this point, Tyson was trying to come up with a way to reveal the demons of the universe without the world breaking out in a riot. That's the last thing they needed right about now.

— — —

"What about this spell?" Sadie asked after about twenty minutes of hopeless searching. Julie peeked at the page that Sadie had her book open to. She had the book open to that page the whole time they were searching but figured if they found another spell to try, the nameless spell would be the last hope spell to try in Julie's mind so she waited.

"It has no name, or description. Just the words that you have to say. And it says you need three people that are skilled in Magic. I don't think that's us."

"It could be worth a try though…" Sadie pushed. She had a gut feeling that this was the spell to go with.

"Okay what do we need for it?"

"Here, you look at it. I don't know how to translate this text." Julie took the spell book out of Sadie's hands and glanced at the page. The text was written in German and only one of the three could pronounce the words even though they had no idea what they were saying, "Well it doesn't say anything about supplies so Sadie can you go get three small white candles and one large one, two red lighters and four blue small rocks?" Sadie left the room.

"I don't know if you should be doing this spell when you don't know what it is or even how to perform it. It's not in English and nameless spells are really dangerous." Tyrone expressed his concern.

"Honestly, Tyrone. Do you think telling me that nameless spells are dangerous is going to scare me out of doing this one? I don't know what it is or what it'll do but if there are consequences, we'll deal with those when they get here. Right now I have a sister to help."

"And if it doesn't help your sister?"

"And if it doesn't help my sister than we'll deal with the consequences after we figure out how to help her.

"You just said there was nothing we could *to* help…now you are just going to do a random nameless spell? What, does not being able to help make you feel helpless? Usually it would make you toughen up and go out to find Kate and Tyson to help them with magic only as a back up plan." Tyrone argued. Julie looked at the spell one more time. *I would do that, but I'm no good at fighting. And if I'm out there, I won't have any supplies to do any spells with. So using magic only as a back up plan wouldn't really work.* Julie thought.

"Look Tyrone. I just have a good feeling about this spell. I know it's probably a huge risk but I feel like we need to complete it quickly. I'm going to go see what's taking Sadie so long." Julie got up from the couch and headed into the supplies closet only to find Sadie struggling to carry all of the supplies she had asked for earlier. Julie took half of the supplies and the two of them went back out to the living room area.

Sadie and Tyrone sat across from Julie, facing her, each with one little blue rock sitting on the palm of their right hand. Julie did the same with her little blue rock after setting up the four candles. The large candle, already lit, sat in the middle of the people triangle and then Julie used it to light the other three candles before putting them around it in a triangle as well. One little candle lined up with each of the three of them. As Julie started saying the first part of the spell, the middle larger candle started floating and spinning, "Besiege den Teufel," She started. Julie continued the spell while not reacting to the larger candle floating and spinning in mid air. Truth was, she didn't know if that was supposed to happen or not, "Das ist meine Aufgabe. Dies ist die Aufgabe, die ich auf die vollständige füllen." Julie closed her eyes and hoped that Tyrone and Sadie would know to keep theirs' open in order to know what to do. Julie didn't understand why she knew the actions to take while performing this spell but she did. She set her blue rock on the flame of the small candle that sat in front of her, "Besiege den Teufel. Das ist mein Ziel. Das ist mein

Wunsch Ich bin bereit, wahr werden zu lassen." She continued as Sadie and Tyrone did the same with their rocks. The spell was almost over and Julie started to feel a pain in her stomach. She didn't know that this was the same pain that Kate was feeling and Sadie and Tyrone didn't have any such pain, "Vielleicht brauche ich Hilfe, ich kann die Hilfe brauchen. Bitte Götter der Götter helfen mir den Weg ich nehmen müssen. Bitte, helfen Götter der Götter mir mein Ziel zu erreichen." The middle candle fell to the floor and started the carpet on fire. Sadie's first reaction was to put out the fire but then she saw that Julie was still doing the spell and that the fire was somehow being controlled by the spell. Julie said the last words of the spell as the pain she felt in her stomach deepened, "Bitte helfen Sie mir komplett meine Aufgabe. bitte helfen mein Wunsch in Erfüllung gehen. Besiege den Teufel."

"What does that translate to?" Sadie asked after Julie gave the okay to talk.

"I have no idea. But it's German, I know that much." Julie answered.

"I can read German so I know what it translates to but that's like the most made up spell I've ever heard. That was so custom to our situation…are you sure you said that right?" Julie looked at the book where the spell was previously and looked back up to Tyson with a frown.

"It disappeared." She announced. They all looked at the blank page in the book, "What did I say, though? What does it translate to?"

"Beat The Devil. That's my job. This is the task which I fill to the full. Beat The Devil. That's my goal. This is my desire I'm ready to play will allow. Maybe I need help, I need help. Please gods of the gods to help me the way I have to take. Please, help me gods of gods reach my goal. Please help me complete my task. please help my wish come true. Beat The Devil."

"But what does that mean? Did it do anything? I don't feel different." As Sadie asked these questions, Julie started to realize what the spell could have meant. But she wasn't sure she had done it in time.

Chapter 15

Sage was laughing at Kate as she bent over in pain the first time. He knew he was going to die before the process was over so he started her transition unnaturally. He was still floating in the air but slowly started coming closer to the couple on the side walk. Kate was bent over and Tyson just stood there next to her for comfort. He knew that the transition was painful, though he didn't know if the unnatural way was different then the normal way to turn someone. Truthfully Tyson didn't know what Kate could be going through. Suddenly Sage stopped laughing. His back bent over backwards as if being cursed again. He hung there in that position for a while, while slowly getting lower and lower until he was only about two yards above the pavement. Sage looked like he was laying on an invisible table with his feet on an invisible floor. Kate looked up briefly between big bursts of pain only to see Sage slam to the ground. There was blood everywhere. Sage's blood; meaning he was dead.

"What just happened!"

"He's dead!" a lady from the nearest house screamed, "Is he dead?" another neighbor asked. Other neighbors were just screaming and calling the police. One called the ambulance which then showed up a couple minutes later along with the press.

— — —

"Did anything happen?" Sadie asked again after a couple minutes of nothing.

"I'm not sure. I don't feel any different. None of us look different. I'm not sure that the spell did anything at all." Julie examined the room to find nothing was different about the room. *What did the spell do?* She asked herself.

"So now do you agree that we should just go physically help them?" Tyrone said with an I-told-you-so look on his face.

"Fine but we aren't going to be able to do anything. I can't see them anymore." Julie knew that by now they wouldn't be able to help Kate and Tyson in any way. Kate was done making her decision and she knew that the three of them waited too long. *Damn it! I should have just listened to Tyrone in the first place. I could have at least been there for Kate when she made the decision. That would have been better than this. At least I think it would've been better. What if she's a vampire already? Oh no!* Julie panicked in her thoughts.

The three of them got their coats and headed out the door, only to find a bunch of demons on the front yard, "What is going *on*?! Julie! I knew that stupid nameless spell was a bad idea!" Sadie screamed. That wasn't true. In fact, Sadie was the primary reason they even tried the nameless spell. All types of demons filled the large front yard. Some of them looked like zombies with how slow they were moving but Julie knew they weren't. There were about a hundred of these random demons filling their lawn and Julie knew of only one way to get rid of any kind of demon. It would only kill them briefly because it was a weak curse but it would let the three of them pass through the demons without fuss. No doubt were these demons sent by Sage to stop any of them from preventing him from becoming free.

"Shush. Let me concentrate." The curse that Julie was about to perform was a curse that Julie had made up quickly in the moment. She just had to concentrate on the demons' heads and they would do exactly what she asked: explode.

"What? What are you going to do?" in the next moment, Sadie and Tyrone were silently standing next to Julie as Julie was concentrating on each of the demons' heads. That's when Sadie and Tyrone both jumped back because the demons' heads just exploded, "Whoa!" they cheered together. But there was no time to explain how that was possible. *If I knew that Julie could do that, we wouldn't need to go out and fight demons, she would just have to make their heads explode and then we could all have a normal life! Why didn't she show us this before?* Sadie complained internally. The three of them ran out to the middle of the yard and then Julie teleported them to where Kate and Tyson stood surrounded by press and the normal looking neighbors. Kate was trying to stop

Tyson from answering any questions. As Julie walked closer, she noticed Sage just lying there on the ground.

Kate bent over in pain. The transition wasn't over yet and she still had most of the major parts left. Tyson had told her through thought that it was going to get a lot more painful. *Wait! So now you can read my mind and I can read your mind?* Kate thought to Tyson. That was part of the transition.

And I can read your thoughts too. Both of yours. So careful about what you think! Tyrone thought from a couple yards away. Kate turned around as Tyrone broke the news to her sisters for her, "She's a vampire. Unnaturally turned but still a vampire." He said quietly.

"Who killed Sage? Kate, was it you?" Sadie asked her sister as she brought her a little away from the press. Kate couldn't respond because of the pain. She shrugged. No one realized that it was the destroyer spell. The nameless spell that Julie had used just because her gut instinct told her to. Tyrone walked over to Julie and put his hand on her shoulder.

"I think it worked, Julie; I think this might have been the work of your spell. I think that's why Sage couldn't have waited to change Kate the natural way. I think that's why she's an unnatural vampire, because you didn't let him complete his freedom." After Sage became free, he had to go through the freedom process. According to the curse that the Sanders' girl ancestors put on Sage, he would have to last for five minutes up in the air in a lot of pain to undo all of the Hell that he had put himself and others through.

"Seriously? My spell worked!" Julie said this a little louder than she meant to and this got the press to rush over to her. Before they got to her, Kate quickly asked the others if they should reveal the vampire race. A lot of people already saw the impossible that night, Kate didn't believe they would be able to just cover this up with a hoax theory. Too many witnesses of the real deal. They all agreed and the press started asking questions.

— — —

"What the *hell* is *that*?" one of the reporters screamed. There was a message, on the sidewalk next to the body of Sage. Kate quickly looked and that's when Sage's body disappeared into thin air. A poof of white smoke replaced the shape of his body as it disappeared. Kate fell to the ground because of the pain and stayed there with Tyson by her side.

"That's a message. We will talk to the press after we figure stuff out. Please just leave us alone until we have all of this under control." Tyrone announced to the people with cameras and microphones.

"What do you have to get under control?" "What happened here today?" "Who was dead on the sidewalk and how did he disappear like that?" "What's going on here?" the reporters wouldn't give up. Tyrone shooed them and said to come back in thirty minutes. They all sighed and went back to their vans but the vans didn't go anywhere and the cameras were still focused on the five of them.

"Can you read that? Does that say what I think it says?" Tyson looked up to the others while holding Kate. He couldn't believe that any of this happened right in front of him.

— — —

"What does it say?" Sadie asked. The message was written in German at first.

Es muss eine dunkle Lord werden oder es wird kein Rennen sein.

After Sadie asked that question, though, the message was erased and rewritten in English. The five of them just stared at the sidewalk as the message rewrote itself where Sage had once laid in his own blood.

There must be a dark lord or there will be no race.

Only Julie knew what this meant. She knew that it was a possibility that there *had* to be a Devil. Now that Sage had made a dimension for torture and for evil souls and evil activity, there was a big probability that Hell had to be active from the moment it was put to use. Meaning there was another Devil and he or she was probably going to be worse than Sage.

— — —

Julie was wearing her only business looking suit for the occasion that was about to start. Sadie was in a dress that went down to her knees and had a beautiful design on it getting more detailed with colors and lines as the design reached the bottom of the dress. In the design there was an encrypted message. Sadie had made the dress herself for an occasion such as a television interview but the message was Julie's idea. Sadie didn't know of the message but it had to do with vampires and demons. No one would ever guess that there was such a message within the design but Julie knew exactly what it meant.

Kate and Tyson matched as though they were each other's date for prom. Kate wore a fancy dress that had ruffles as it got to the ground and she wore a silver necklace that Tyson bought for her. Tyson wore a tuxedo with a yellow shirt underneath to match Kate's yellow dress. He wore his normal fake-silver chain around his neck and a fake-silver watch he just bought two days previously before the big event.

Tyrone couldn't believe that they were about to announce the existence of the demonic race. Was it their choice to do so? He worried that the leaders of their world would come around and kill them or punish them for making such a big decision without any other demons knowing about it.

"So the last time we talked with the bunch of you, I believe Kate was in a lot of pain," Kate frowned and nodded, "and there was a man's body lying on the ground. Then the man disappeared literally into thin air and there was a message one the ground in another language." Laura, the TV host recapped the last day's events, "Can any of you tell us what the message said and what the message meant? And what language was it in, do you know?"

"I know what it means." Julie announced to the TV host, "It was in German and changed to English. It said 'There must be a dark lord or there will be no race.' It's a warning to us because we killed Sage."

"And who is Sage, exactly?"

"Sage...well, Laura, it's a long story. We would like to break some news to everyone. It's going to be hard to accept. Is that allowed? Can we..."

"Yes! Of course!" the host cheered.

"Humans are not the only beings that live on Earth. And I don't mean to sound like I'm announcing the existence of like animals and stuff. What I mean to say is Hell is real and a *human* named Sage created it as a different dimension. At first it was for him to just escape to when he needed a break from the Earth's people but he turned it into an evil place of vengeance and became evil within himself as well. Sage eventually called himself The Devil because he became so powerful. He named his dimension Hell because of the reference that comes with The Devil being in Hell. It was his own name for himself but it caught on with the demons around him. Sage was a human being like you and me that played with the black magic. Don't get me wrong, magic is an amazing thing; to a point. Have too much power and you'll get overthrown with greed for more power. Our family's ancestors cursed Sage. They trapped him in his own dimension of torture. The curse was not very thought through and wasn't the best idea but it allowed Sage freedom only after he *collected* six hundred and sixty-six souls. This is why the number 666 kind of represents The Devil." Julie started.

"What do you mean by collect?" the lady asked.

"We mean collect. A human without a soul is technically dead but Sage made it so he wasn't actually technically 'killing' the victims of his curse. He made them the walking dead. Our ancestors thought that Sage wouldn't be able to go through with killing that many innocent humans but they were wrong." Sadie continued.

"Vampires. Tyson Michaels is a vampire and so is Tyrone Dean. More times than not, Sage made it so the victim either had the choice of dying or becoming part of the undead world. And most chose to be undead; because they were afraid to die." Kate said, "I'm not one hundred percent sure about this but when Sage tricked me into giving him the six hundred and sixty sixth soul, he didn't get the chance to change me. But the deal with him was that I give him my soul and in return he doesn't put Hell on Earth."

"Ooo! Very Heroic of you." She commented.

"Yes, thank you. But because Julie's spell worked, Sage knew he was going to die and unnaturally turned me into a vampire. There are some differences between me and Tyson and Tyrone though."

"Well? Like what?"

"We're not sure yet. I've only been a vampire for a day." Kate laughed revealing that she had fangs, "One difference that I have noticed, though, is that I don't crave human blood yet. Usually a new vampire needs a couple days worth of fresh blood. They crave it so much they can't control who they are drinking from. This blood lust hasn't hit me yet but we are taking precautions."

"So, this next question is for Julie specifically. What are you?"

"I am a witch but that's a title not a species; I'm human. Like Sage, I play with the magic. I lean more towards the white magic, not the black magic. The difference is good versus evil, basically. But I don't really want to get into the magic. That can be saved for another time." Julie stated.

"Okay. Sadie, now I have a question for you. What do you do for your family. Kate is the leader, Julie is the witch. What are you?"

"I can answer that!" Tyrone cut in.

"Oh! Okay." Laura said smiling. Laura scooted slightly away from the group that she was interviewing. So slightly that only the three vampires on stage could tell that she moved. The three of them could tell that Laura was a little uncomfortable having three vampires next to her. Kate and Tyrone thought it was funny but Tyson found it annoying to be seen as a monster, even though it was to be expected.

"Sadie is the smarts and the strength. I personally think that if Sadie hadn't said anything about seeing that spell that we found…we were looking for something to help Kate and Tyson out but Sadie is the one that found the spell…" Tyrone couldn't choose the words.

"What Tyrone is trying to say is that Sadie is the reason we did that spell meaning Sadie is the reason Kate and Tyson are still here with us and *Sadie* is the reason Hell is…" Suddenly Julie was gone. In the middle of her sentence on broadcast TV that was being shown around the world, her seat became empty with a poof.

"Did she just do that herself? Did Julie just show us a *magic* trick?"

"No! Julie wouldn't do that in the middle of a sentence. Something happened!" Sadie yelled.

"Well guys, we're almost out of time. Any last comments?"

"Witches exist!" Kate started, "Vampires are among us! And The Devil," the others joined in, "has been destroyed!"

The TV show ended and Kate started freaking out about what happened too. Tyrone and Tyson didn't seem all that surprised which made everything more suspicious.

ABOUT THE AUTHOR

Skyler DeGrote is a full time college student pursuing a degree in Advertising. She lives on campus while classes are in session and moves back home for the summers. When home, Skyler lives with her parents and her cat, Sarabi.

She has enjoyed writing fiction novels for many years and is currently working on the next book in The Soul Collection.

www.ingramcontent.com/pod-product-compliance
Lightning Source LLC
Chambersburg PA
CBHW050938120626
46552CB00001B/262